THE RACQUET

The Racquet

OR

Viajes por America Lejana
by César-Agosto Villaseñor M.
(as translated from the Spanish)

by George Hitchcock

STORY LINE PRESS
1993

© 1993 by George Hitchcock
First American Printing

All rights reserved. No part of this book may be reproduced in any form or by any electronic or mechanical means including information storage and retrieval systems without permission in writing from the publisher, except by a reviewer.

ISBN: 0-93425754-X

Published by Story Line Press, Inc., Three Oaks Farm, Brownsville, OR 97327

This publication was made possible thanks in part to the generous support of the Nicholas Roerich Museum, the Andrew W. Mellon Foundation, and our individual contributors.

TABLE OF CONTENTS

A Piece of Cake	7
A Man of Principle	12
The Road to Poulsbo	18
A Matter of Metabolism	26
Purification	34
Man of Action	41
Family Affairs	48
Weekending in Oregon	57
Urim and Thummim	63
Some Failed Connections	70
I Get My Racquets Back	77
Phyllis	82
Albert	89
I Become a Tycoon	97
Champion at Last	103
Some Farewells	110
Enzel	116
Looking for Captain Jack	123
In Which I Hit Bottom	131
Myron and Sybil	135
Some Sumatran Tigers	141
I Meet Old Friends	149
A Roman Tragedy	158
A Tempting Offer	163
Up in the Air	169
Blown Away	173
Mr. Fawcett's Empire	179
No Bingo, No Obligation	186
Unexpected Drop Shots	191
On the Road Again	197
Homecomings	204
Marcantonio	209
What Happened Afterward	216

A Piece of Cake

"Always excepting the British," said Mr. Wilfred Robertson-Bentley, "you can take it for granted that Europeans who end up here are strictly *en route.*"

"The band is going to play *it* again, Wilfred dear," Mrs. Robertson-Bentley announced.

"Shit," her husband said without any particular affect. But we all three stood up and faced the rotunda at the opening notes of *God Save the Queen*. Only when the orchestra returned to some anesthetized tango did he continue: "They're either here expecting to get a visa or else they're perennially—perhaps I should say terminally—disappointed. You can read which by their faces."

"Wilfred is quite right," Mrs. Robertson-Bentley said in a tone which seemed to anticipate and confound contradiction.

"But I'm not European," I objected.

"Your skin is white—"

"Not exactly," his wife interrupted. "He has a delicious tan."

"—so you count for a European." Serenely, he ignored the footnote. "And from your high spirits and *naïveté* I should say you haven't been waiting long. Tell me, Agosto, have you ever been in the United States?"

"No, sir, this will be my first trip."

"Not even in the transit lounge in godforsaken-utterly-plasticized-Miami-Florida?"

We all laughed dutifully. "Not even then," I said.

"A great country. Don't get me wrong. Fair is fair.

The United States are a great country."

"Wilfred doesn't go there any more," Mrs. Bentley explained. "He finds their tax laws very unjust and, well, discriminatory."

"That's the word," her husband said. "The very word I would have used. Dis-crim-in-at-ory."

We were seated on a sunny afternoon in early spring in the grounds of the Empress Hotel in Victoria, surrounded in equal proportions by waiters and tourists. The wind was blowing briskly amidst the fleecy clouds overhead and spasmodically disturbing the table linen. On the lawn behind us three North Americans in flowing scarves and white flannels were chortling over croquet. I had known the Robertson-Bentleys for only twenty-four hours but already they seemed interested in my future. Plans were in the air. Perhaps it's because I am a good listener and am genuinely respectful of older people but today I was particularly agreeable because I hadn't eaten all day and was stealthily destroying the prosciutto rolls and openfaced endive sandwiches the waiters kept slipping in front of me. Foraging, I called it.

"The British, on the other hand, come here to die in the most convincing replica of an Edwardian town that Canadian nostalgia can possibly construct. No matter that the original never existed, the copy authenticates it. Have you been to the Butchart Gardens?"

"Not yet, sir," I said. "I just got here Thursday."

"More or less out of funds?"

"Wilfred!" But instead of nudging her husband in reproof, as perhaps she intended, Mrs. Robertson-Bentley pressed her knee against mine under the tablecloth.

"All right, all right," her husband said amiably. "Mustn't get personal. But if I were a punting man, which I'm not, one would get you ten I'm not far wide of the mark, eh, Agosto?"

"I have a couple of travellers' cheques but not very much else," I admitted.

"And the banks are closed till after the holidays?"

"I'm afraid so, sir."

"Let me advance you a few dollars." Mr. Robertson-Bentley took out a prosperous looking notecase. "I'm afraid though it will have to be in Canadian currency." I thanked him without overdoing it; I didn't want him to get the impression that money was all that important to me.

"Now for the roses!" said his wife. "The first cutting should be just ready." And as, with a heavily ringed hand on my arm, she steered me across the parking lot to their Mercedes, she added in a throaty whisper, "I think Wilfred has a job for you. He has really taken to you, Agosto."

And I had taken to the Robertson-Bentleys, too, or at least to their life-style which appeared to be compounded of money, fine cars, good food and generosity; in short, all the qualities I had always imagined in upperclass Americans and had dreamed of sharing with them. Only they weren't Americans at all. What were they, then? Mrs. Bentley had literally brushed across me on the hotel tennis court and I had taken her immediately for an English woman—a hard trim figure, newly-laundered tennis skirt displaying good legs, a turquoise headband keeping her pageboy in place and her mouth set in a very earnest smile that made me think of the Sisters of Intolerable Mercy, a smile which lets you know how horrible the world really is but we're going to be brave about it, aren't we? And her husband, despite his digs at the British, was, with his pink skin, clipped red moustache and tweeds, almost the prototype of the Anglo sporting type I used to see at the Buenos Aires Racquet Club when I shagged balls there. Perhaps he was South African or a New Zealander—my ear wasn't expert enough to tell—but he had fine manners (I've always admired that), leisure, wit, money, and a fatherly interest in me. His wife's interest was definitely more ambiguous but that was a challenge, too. In short, I was happy in this new friendship and ready as always for what fate might bring.

The job, too, turned out to be easy, yet with just enough mystery to appeal to my romantic side. As we walked up and down the oyster-shell pathways between the rose trees Mr. Robertson-Bentley explained to me that his wife's young cousin kept a sport-fishing launch across the straits in Washington state. He had a taste, it seemed, for a particular Canadian smoked salmon. "Of course," he explained, "there's plenty of smoked salmon in Washington but the quality's inferior. The Canadian stuff would drive it off the market if it weren't for the ruinous duties the Yanks put on it." This was where I came in. Mr. Robertson-Bentley would buy me a ticket—"round-trip of course so you can say you are just going shopping in Seattle"—on the international ferry to Port Angeles. He would also provide me with a duffel-bag full of Grade-A Vancouver Island smoked fish and all I had to do was drop it overboard as we passed a certain buoy at the entrance to Port Angeles harbor. His wife's cousin—"a topping fellow and a first-class forward wing, you'd love him if you could meet him"—would do the rest.

"A piece of cake," he summarized. "You can't miss the buoy. It's the second one on the right of the channel, fresh-painted orange, and on a line with the boat-yard derrick."

"But—"

"Yes?"

"Won't the salmon be spoiled by the sea water?"

"Leave that to Hubert. He'll have the bag out of there before you can say Jack Robinson. And naturally, every package is wrapped in waterproofing." He paused and with his silver cigar-knife neatly snipped off a rosebud and put it in his lapel. "Well, what do you think?"

"I'm not sure of one thing, sir . . . "

"Yes?" a sudden cold glint appeared in his eye.

". . . whether I want to come back to Victoria . . . just yet."

"Then cash in the return and off with you to Seattle. You've done your bit. The rest is up to Hubert."

"Oh yes!" Mrs. Robertson-Bentley said gaily, as if the mere thought of her stalwart young soccer-playing cousin had brightened an afternoon which was, after some intermittent sun, growing cloudy and dull. "Hubert will take care of all that."

"I would be much obliged if you would help us out, Agosto."

"*Como no?*" I said.

"What?"

"That's Spanish," I explained, "for how could I possibly refuse."

So we shook hands all around and went into the Rose Garden Arms for a drink. Of whiskey this time.

A MAN OF PRINCIPLE

It was only later, when I had boarded the ferry *Orcas* (Spanish, incidentally, for the killer whale) for Port Angeles, that I began to feel nervous. The ferry company was called the Black Ball Line, which wasn't a good omen. Then the canvas bag of smoked salmon was a lot bulkier than I had anticipated. It weighed at least thirty kilograms and I realized it wasn't going to be easy dropping it overboard without attracting attention.

"Suppose it sinks," I said to Mr. Robertson-Bentley as the both of us tugged it out of the trunk of his Mercedes.

But he was breezily confident. "That's not an option, old bean. Did you ever hear of fish *sinking* in the ocean? Not bloody likely. They're designed to float. One of God's little tricks. There now, boost it up on your shoulder. Besides, they're all dehydrated. Once you get used to the weight you'll find it lighter than you think."

Still, with the addition of my own luggage and tennis racquets I felt awkward and badly loaded down. I staggered into the forward lounge and left the gear while I went back to the taffrail and waved goodbye to the Robertson-Bentleys. She waved back with her turquoise scarf while he shouted something which sounded like "Don't leaveitalone," although the *Orcas*'s whistle and the noisy seagulls made it impossible to be certain. It had begun to rain. I felt sure I would never see them again.

When I got back to the lounge everything was just

as I had left it, only someone was in my seat. He got up at once.

"Excuse me, I didn't realize this was occupied."

"It's all right," I said, "I'll take another." There were very few passengers.

"No, no, that wouldn't be fair."

"It doesn't matter."

"But it does to me. I never wish to impose." And he moved into the next seat but one and neatly folded his overcoat and placed it between us.

"Thank you."

"Ah," he said, "you mustn't thank me for doing what is, after all, morally obligatory." He was a birdlike little man with a porkpie hat and very thick glasses through which he watched me intently.

"This crossing takes two hours and fifty-five minutes," he announced in a confidential tone. Obviously he felt that his self-sacrifice had earned him conversational rights. "When the weather is good you can see the Olympic range which is usually snow-covered at this time of the year. Of course today that's not possible."

Like a *buho*, I thought, a little hedge-owl staring out of a thicket.

"Excuse me," I said rising, "I have to find the W.C."

Helpfully, he indicated the direction.

"You can leave that sack."

"I'm afraid not." I hoisted it on my shoulders.

"It will be perfectly safe. I'll keep an eye on it."

The hell you will, I said to myself and went out on the foredeck. The rain was driving down, the deck was slippery and it was impossible to see anything either fore or aft. The sea was a dirty green and the current in the straits seemed to be running out; here and there I saw a nasty tide-rip. The deckhands in their yellow oilskins were coiling and uncoiling wet ropes that looked like sea-snakes. It was a depressing day.

El Buho was still there when I got back, only now he was shuffling a well-worn pack of cards.

"Would you care to join me in a game of gin rummy?" he inquired.

I was reluctant to get involved with him but I saw no good way to refuse so he dealt me seven cards and we began to play. For an hour we played in almost complete silence. He played well, with a much better knowledge of the combinations than I, yet he never offered to gamble, which was a relief. All the while the *Orcas* ploughed ahead through curtains of gray, rocking, shivering, and gasping as if it hurt it to breathe the wet channel air.

After winning six games in a row the Owl put down the cards and said solemnly, "I am a Christian."

Since he obviously wanted to talk I showed a polite interest. "Have you been—how do they say it up here?—born again?"

"Unfortunately, no. I am a Christian by conviction but I have not received the gift of faith."

I said that was too bad and added that it must be very uncomfortable not to believe wholeheartedly in what your intellect told you was true.

"It is very painful." I could see the suffering in his eyes. "There is nothing I would rather do than lead my life according to the Gospels, yet here I am, steeped in sin, playing cards with a boy young enough to be my own son. Doesn't that surprise you? That a Christian would play the devil's game?"

I said that I was only surprised that he played it so well.

"Yes," he said bitterly, "I am ashamed of that, too. It would be best not to play at all, that would be the

Gospel path. But then if I must sin I ought to do it badly. Showing off my skill is the sin of Pride and I know I'll be punished for it." He sighed. "I make my living selling siding and flashing—"

"What are they?" I was genuinely mystified.

"Materials to keep the weather out. Or in, as the case may be. Aluminum, redwood, pine. But that's not my point. The salesmen in siding and flashing are a sharp lot, ask anyone, not a Gospel Christian in a hundred. Yet I have to tell you—" and here he rapped me on the knee—"I *enjoy* getting the better of them! Yes, and the customers, too, who are mostly a lot of silly sheep living in fear that the termites are going to eat their walls and windows for breakfast. I want to get the better of them, too. How's that for a Christian?"

I said I thought it was just fine to have a winner's attitude if you weren't dishonest about it.

"No, no!" He raised his voice. "Competitive pride is evil—it's the way of the devil. Read the Gospels. Read the Sermon on the Mount—it's all spelled out there."

But he had touched me, a competitive athlete, on a sore point. "There's nothing wrong with wanting to win," I said hotly. "Look at Thomas Edison, look at Simón Bolívar—where would they have been if they hadn't played to win?"

"I don't judge what others do. I only speak my own principles."

But his lofty tone infuriated me. "It's all right for you North Americans to talk about your principles," I said loudly. "You'll excuse me for saying it, but you already have everything, so you have plenty of time to think about what's right and wrong. But we in the poor countries don't have that luxury. We *have* to play to win. You can afford your Gospel principles—we can't."

"I hadn't meant to make it a political question," he

protested.

But I saw my opportunity to get rid of him and I wouldn't let him evade me.

"Everything is political!" I exploded. "That's the trouble with you Protestants. You think you can compartmentalize life—this little box for making money, this one for sex, here politics, over there religion, that box for charity, this one for making war—well, it won't work, not with me. I can see right through it and it . . . *disgusts* me!"

He seemed shattered. But before he could answer I charged out of the lounge, dragging my gear behind me. The truth is, I enjoy getting angry. It clears the arteries, as my father used to say. And of course when I make myself angry I only half believe what I'm saying—I'm riding the crest of a wave, trying to keep my balance any way I can. Later I'm sorry, but then *that's* a wave too, and there are ways of riding it. The chief thing is to stay alive, really alive, and always ready for the next game.

On deck I practiced my off-loading. I found that by slinging the sack over my shoulder and letting it rest on the railing I was in position to launch it with a slight nudge of one shoulder. Ideally, it would look like an accident. Of course, there was a chance that the sack might be sucked into the propellor and hacked to pieces, but that was Hubert's responsibility not mine. Meanwhile, I stood in the damp sea-spray, waiting. There were no other passengers brave enough to be out there. A deckhand came by and asked if I was seasick. I was, a little, but denied it. The fresh air was bracing, I told him.

And in due time the United States appeared, dimly, on the horizon, the *Orcas* hooted at the oncoming shore and the first channel-buoy bobbed past. To be followed, right on schedule, by the orange buoy. When we were opposite it I nudged the bag, it fell with a modest and almost inaudible splash, and drifted safely away. No one was looking. It was, as my employer said, a piece of cake. Out there in the choppy green water beyond the marker I could distinctly see a speed-boat idling about. Whoever was in it, I mentally saluted them and wished them good luck.

As I waited to disembark *El Buho* showed up again, very damp and sad-looking. He apologized for his "rudeness."

"No," I said. "I am the one who ought to apologize." Suddenly I felt lighthearted and in a completely forgiving mood. "It was wrong of me to lecture you."

"No, no, it was the other way around."

We shook hands. His car, it seemed, was on the lower deck and he would be happy to take me as far as Seattle. Where was I going?

"To see America," I said gaily. "My sister is getting married in San Diego on the third of September. Until then—*quién sabe?*" I was in wonderful spirits again.

But ahead was yet another trial—the United States Customs.

The Road to Poulsbo

"You are approaching customs inspection," a recording informed me. "Take a number, please, and be seated until you are called." I took a ticket from the dispenser. It was Number 163 which certainly suggested a long wait but it was over-stamped, "Numeration out of use. Proceed directly to inspection." I got in line and shuffled along, kicking my luggage ahead of me toward a formidable looking black inspector. From time to time the loudspeaker repeated its futile message. It reminded me comfortingly of South America; apparently not everything worked in the United States either.

I was jarred from these thoughts by loud barking. A German shepherd, barely restrained on its leash by a stout female, was heading for me. It growled, bared its teeth, then sniffed and slobbered over my suitcase as if it were full of porterhouse steaks. The stout lady promptly X'ed my luggage with blue chalk. What that meant I was to discover when I got to the Guardian of the Gates.

He began amiably enough. "Where have you been, sir?"

"Kyoto, sir."

"Where's that?"

"Japan, sir."

"Are you Japanese?"

I showed him my passport with its tourist visa.

"Uruguay?"

"Yes, sir."

"I didn't think you looked Japanese." He was visibly more relaxed now. "I have a brother who's in Honduras.

In the army."

I've had enough dealings with officials to know better than make any witty retorts, so I restrained myself and merely nodded.

"Any fruits, vegetables or meat products?"

"No, sir."

"Been on a farm anytime in the last thirty days?"

"No, sir."

I think with this he was about to pass me when his eyes lit on the blue chalkmarks.

"Where'd you get these?" He was all cold efficiency now; friendly chit-chat was over.

"I think your dog took an irrational dislike to me, sir."

"Open your suitcase, mister," he snapped.

I did so and he poured my clothes and shaving things all over the counter. He went through everything piece by piece and then held the empty bag upside down and shook it. A few grains of Japanese beach sand fell out. He wetted his forefinger and tasted it.

"It's sand, sir."

"I'm not an idiot," he said sternly. "I can tell that."

"Of course you can, sir."

"You'd be surprised what people try to sneak through, mister. What's in here?" He picked up my tennis case as if it were a venomous snake.

"My tennis racquets, sir."

"Open the case."

I did so.

"Ah!" he said triumphantly. "There's more than one. In point of fact, three. Are you in the licensed import business?"

"No, sir. I'm a tennis player."

"A what?"

"A professional tennis player. I was in Japan playing

exhibition matches, Sir." (Losing most of them, I might have added.)

He took the racquets up one by one, tested the strings, peered down the handles and hefted them for weight and resilience. They definitely interested him.

"I could have this here handle cut off to see what's inside. That's within my power. You wouldn't much like that, would you, mister?"

I said I definitely wouldn't. "They're Heads and very expensive. You might try X-raying them first if you think I'm silly enough to carry anything in them."

"I might, I might," he said and stuffed the racquets back in their carrying-bag. "Actually, that was just a psychological gambit."

"To prove what?"

"Just testing responses, mister. The question don't mean anything by itself but we like to see how the subject responds. Whether he fits the profile or not."

"And my response, did it fit?"

"It fell within the normal parameters," he said in his best officialese. "You can put your sweaters back, mister, you're on your way."

"I'm cleared?"

"You can thank your lucky stars the dog was having an off day. And, mister—"

"Yes?"

"I'd buy a raincoat if I was you. You've just entered the sovereign state of Washington."

And the United States of America, I thought jubilantly. Outside the terminal *El Buho* was waiting for me, his glasses completely rain-misted but the same friendly, apologetic smile on his lips.

"Any difficulty?" he asked.

"It was the dog that held me up. I think he smelled fish."

"They'll do that," El Buho said wisely. "Dogs have very keen olfactory organs."

We got into his car. It was an old black Cadillac of the sort undertakers take the family to the cemetery in. Or *caudillos* drive from an airport. You know the kind. I felt like hammering the windows to see if they were bullet-proofed.

"Where's the big canvas bag? I hope you didn't forget it."

"I threw it in the ocean," I said casually.

He digested this in silence. But I was ready for him; I had a prepared version I was proud of and didn't want to waste.

"It was a mission, a memorial mission. On my part."

"Yes?" The Cadillac purred and took the road for Seattle.

"For Raúl. My best friend. He was killed last month on Fujiyama. It was about this time of day, just getting dark. We were rappelling—"

"Excuse me. I don't understand—"

"Descending a rock face on a rope. There was a crevasse and, well...Raúl didn't make it . . . ."

"A tragic accident? A mishap!"

"Washington was his home," I continued quickly. "He began his climbing here in the Olympic Mountains. Before he died he made me promise to throw his climbing gear into the sea off his native shore."

"So that bag—?"

"Held his ropes, his boots, pitons, climbing breeches, everything." I was reckless and enthusiastic now as I described Raúl's last moments in my arms—after all, the evidence was flotsam in the Straits of Juan de Fuca, I was over the border, and I didn't much care whether *El Buho* believed my tale or not.

Not that I had to worry. He was utterly absorbed in

the moral implications of the drama.

"Did you feel yourself responsible for his death?"

"But I wasn't."

"You were climbing together."

I admitted that.

"Perhaps you were roped together. You might possibly have saved him when he slipped. That instant when you knew he was falling, what did you think then? I should have blamed myself. But perhaps you are different. How old are you?"

"Twenty-two."

"That's it," he said with a sigh. "Each generation is different. You're young, guilt doesn't weigh as heavily, you recuperate faster. No, I don't blame you, no doubt you did what you could." He stared for a few moments through the slip-slop of the windshield wipers. "And I do think it was really very . . . well, beautiful of you to make this trip to memorialize your friend. Very beautiful and caring."

We fell silent. I could think of nothing more to say and I was beginning to feel shame. Not as he supposed over the mythical Raúl lost in the snows of Fujiyama, but for tricking this decent, kindly man and provoking his emotions with my falsehoods.

Night was falling. We drove through the town of Sequim ("They call it Squim," my driver explained) past oyster-sheds and stunted pines, steak houses and failing garages. Suddenly he pulled over onto the shoulder.

"What is it?"

He turned sharp and decisive. "This is as far as you ride with me, my friend."

"What's the matter?"

"Look." Two hundred meters ahead I saw a bank of revolving red and blue lights. "It's a road-block. You can cut through the forest and get back to the road on the other side. Be quick about it."

"But why would they stop me? I have a visa, I'm here legally."

"It's not you they want," he said fiercely. "Now do as I say and don't argue. If I get through I'll wait for you on the other side. But go. Quickly!"

I ran off without another word. After stumbling and falling a few times I found a farm road that ran parallel and fifteen minutes later I emerged on the main road. I walked back a hundred meters until I could plainly see the bank of police cars. The old Cadillac was there too but I saw no sign of my friend and, since there seemed to be at least a dozen highway patrolmen gathered around the barricade, I decided the path of wisdom lay in the other direction and began jogging away down the wet asphalt. And *El Buho*? Any moment I expected him to overtake me but he didn't. In fact, I never saw him again. Was he a murderer, arsonist, child molester or revolutionary? To this day I don't know. I searched the Seattle newspapers the next day; there was no mention of any manhunt or road blockade, not an arrest reported at Sequim or on the North Coast, not a hint of my owlish companion's round face and porkpie hat. In short, he had vanished utterly and irrevocably. Only later did I realize, that such disappearances are far from uncommon in the vast draughty spaces of North America.

After walking and jogging two hours through a scrubland of dunes and jackpine, I came to the lights of Paul Bunyan's Last Chance Lounge. It stood alone in the forest under a huge carved sign showing a bearded giant carrying a log on his shoulder. I was wet and miserable. There seemed nothing to do but go to Mr. Bunyan, whoever he was, and ask for his hospitality. But as I stood, irresolute, in the parking-lot the door to the Lounge flew open and a tall thin man with muddy Levis and a cowboy hat came stamping down the porch steps toward me. "Mothahfuckas, mothahfuckas," he said to himself without any particular conviction. I stepped out of the shadows and asked him for a ride. He seemed startled.

"Who the fuck are you?"

"I'm a tennis player," I stammered. I was drenched and shivering.

"Where you going?"

"South," I said. "Toward Seattle."

He grinned. "Got rained out, huh?" I agreed. "You a foreigner or something?"

Yes, I said, something like that.

He thought this over, then barked, "Well, get in, don't stand there in the rain like a fuckin idjut," and when I moved to the passenger side of his pick-up he said, "No, no, no, no, no" more times than I could count and pointed me to the driver's seat. "You better take the helm tonight, old buddy." He passed me the car-keys. They were attached to a real scorpion set in clear plastic. "Poulsbo. Put it down right in the fuckin center of Poulsbo."

I didn't know where Poulsbo was and there was no use asking the cowboy because he immediately fell asleep. So I started the motor and drove off down the road where in time thanks to the efficient signposting of North American highway engineers it became clear enough that Poulsbo was a town somewhere ahead in the night. The rain was clearing, the cab of the truck was warm, and I've always loved driving. Anyway, I had successfully passed the ordeals at the frontier and was now safely in the United States at last. Even my concern over *El Buho* began to recede; whatever had happened to him I felt sure he would be drawing a moral lesson from it.

His battered hat down over his eyes and spittle trickling from the corners of his mouth, my companion snored on steadily. But he snapped awake and upright the instant I slowed down to enter Poulsbo.

"That's it!" he shouted. "Stop right here. End of the line."

I pulled up along the Viking Motel ($18.95 Truckers Rate).

"You had a good nap," I said, to be sociable.

"Nap?" he bristled. "I been awake all the time, watching you drive. You don't think I'd let some Mex run off with this here Datsun, do you?"

I assured him I had no such intention.

"Nothing personal, old buddy, nothing personal. But this country's full of fuckin bandits and you gotta keep your fuckin eyes open, that's all."

He glared at me and snatched away the keys and their plasticized scorpion. I got out, took my luggage from the truck, went into the Viking, took a room and a lukewarm shower, and slept until eleven the next morning. I had arrived.

A Matter of Metabolism

It was a lovely blowy spring morning. I had just come off the center court at the Bainbridge Island Tennis Club where I was playing a warm-up match with the resident pro. His name was Steve Ladak and I was staying in an old clapboard house behind the club as his guest. I am ranked 224 in the world computer ratings and while that number certainly isn't very intimidating on the professional circuit it was big news at Bainbridge Island, particularly as Steve, with only a local ranking, had just taken a set 6-4. I am nothing if not tactful. Later on when our friendship was on a more solid footing I planned to rev up the motors.

"Gus," Steve said, "this is Sabrina. Sabrina Fridley, Agosto Villaseñor." I shook hands with a slender blue-eyed girl with straight, taffy-colored hair. I knew she had been watching me intently from the sidelines—it's one of those things you pick up on if you're at all sensitive to women. Now she stared at me directly and unabashedly.

"You've got it bad," she said with concern. "Does it itch much?"

From that moment I hated her.

Two nights before, trying to avoid the roadblock, I had fallen into a thicket of venomous plants the North Americans call poison oak although they aren't oak at all but some sort of sumac. My neck, one side of my face and both fore-arms had broken out with an ugly red rash. The pharmacist in Winslow had sold me a pink ointment called Caladryl so now I was doubly disfigured. I am vain about my physique, I admit it, and this girl's tasteless remarks weren't calculated to make me feel any better.

"It's not good to sweat," she went on. "It just spreads it. And if you use the club towels to dry off with you ought to throw them in the washer right away."

"Thanks for the advice," I said coldly.

She was cheerfully oblivious to my sarcasm. "You're from South America, aren't you? That's where they make poultices out of *maté* or *yerba buena*—they draw the poisons from your body in twenty-four hours."

"I live in Montevideo," I said. "It's a big city and we don't consult witch-doctors there."

It was useless; irony was lost on her; she just smiled and kept on coming: "A country that doesn't respect its shamans must be really unhappy."

"Don't worry, Sabrina," Steve put in. "It's already past the virulent stage."

"Let's play," I said grimly. We went back on the court. I called on my tournament serve and took the next two sets, 6-1, 6-2. In the heat of play I forgot all about Sabrina Fridley but when I came off she was still there.

"You have a lot of aggression stored up, don't you?" she observed cheerfully and, before I could answer, switched the subject: "Do you know anything about motorboats?"

"Something."

"Will you come boating with us—my father, my cousin and me—tomorrow afternoon? We're taking lunch and will picnic on that island."

"Where?"

"There in the Sound." She pointed to the south—there in the inlet below us was a small islet, thick with feathery trees and fringed by a scallop of sand. "I'll feel safer with someone aboard who can steer. Father and Cappy are dunderheads."

"All right," I said. "I'll come."

I think she sensed my reluctance for she immediately threw in, as if it were additional bait, "And I promise not to say anything about your poison oak."

"Promise?"

"Cross my heart."

*

Her father was a fussy, nervous little man whose glasses were anchored to his neck with a rawhide thong; as I was to find out, he collected Indian artifacts. His manners, at least toward me, were graceful and elegant but underlying his charm I sensed futility and despair, a despair which might never find outward expression but was always there like a deep pool which shimmers and festers at the same time. He sat primly in the back of the launch, the picnic basket balanced on his bony knees.

Her cousin I didn't like at all. He was pink, scrubbed, overweight and seemed to float in a light mist of cologne. At first I thought him stupid but then I changed my mind and guessed that his air of impenetrable self-satisfaction was, like the cologne, an affectation to protect a too-easily bruised ego. His conversational offerings were of unadulterated sarcasm.

As we approached the island Sabrina and I kicked off our espadrilles and jumped overboard to bring the launch in. The two men stepped ashore carefully, even daintily, and Mr. Fridley spread a cloth on the sand before lowering the lunch basket.

"The ants will be utterly overjoyed," the cousin said, making a big thing out of the *utterly*. He had very white teeth and a small yellow moustache.

We went for a barefoot walk, Sabrina and I. I was beginning to get over my aversion to her.

"How old are you?" she asked.
"Twenty-two."
"You look younger," she said. And then added, "Although yesterday when I met you you looked a lot older than that."
"I *am* younger today. Perhaps it's being with you."
"Don't bullshit me," she said bluntly and stared intently at me with her slightly protuberant corn-flower blue eyes. "What do you want most out of life?"
"Freedom," I said without thinking; suddenly my mind seemed to function badly.
"Freedom for what?"
"Just freedom."
She pouted, a very attractive little *moue*. "It has to be freedom *for* something. Freedom all by itself is just boredom."
"All right, freedom to move about, to travel. To drive a fast car, an Alfa-Romeo, down a long straight road with palm trees on either side."
"And at the end?"
"Of —?"
"The road, silly. What's there?"
"I don't really know." I laughed. "Perhaps because with me it's more important just to keep out of the ditch."
"Are you ambitious?"
"Not really."
After a moment she said, "I think you are."
"Perhaps a little. I'm not sure. I'd like to play tennis better."
"Then you're ambitious." She made it sound as if she were summarizing a ledger. "Have you ever been in love?"
"I don't think so."
"If you don't know, then you haven't been."

"Then I suppose I haven't. I'm too preoccupied with myself, I know that."

"Are you afraid of it?"

"Falling in love?"

"Yes."

"Not at all," I said bravely. "*Que será será.*"

"I think you are," she said, still without releasing me from those incredibly blue eyes. And it was true I was trembling, though at the time I felt sure it wasn't from fear.

"Luncheon!" her father called from down the beach.

"Don't be rude to Cappy," Sabrina whispered as we drew near them. "I know he's an absolute worm but he's very sensitive and picks up on everything."

"I'll try to be decent."

She squeezed my hand gratefully.

"Oh nature walks! Oh blissful education!" the worm rhapsodized in a clear tenor.

The lunch was wonderful—chicken still hot from the *rotisserie* spit, a crisp spinach salad, French wine, a heavy-crusted bread that the cousin tore apart barehanded, Greek olives, pickled mushrooms and cold mussels in vinaigrette. Afterwards, as I lay on the sand fishing wrinkled black olives out of a jar, I watched Sabrina. Her blonde hair was quite straight and showed no trace of the hair-dresser; her face was flawless except for her improbably blue eyes which were perhaps a little too prominent, and her figure was that of a boy more than a grown woman. She exuded cleanliness and as I watched a little iridescent bead of sweat trickle down her upper lip I began to feel, if not exactly lust, at least an intense physical curiosity.

Her father, dressed as if ready for the deck-chair at an old-fashioned yacht club in striped linen jacket, white duck trousers and a ribboned straw hat, was talking about mussels, the one proper hour to pluck them from the rocks and the few acceptable ways one might prepare them. He seemed to know an immense amount about foods of every country and description—it was strange that with all that knowledge he remained so thin and wispy. Eating brought him *expertise* but not, I thought, much enjoyment.

The cousin, on the other hand, had eaten lustily and now, with unbuttoned vest and straw hat shading his eyes against the late afternoon light, lay on his back in a mossbank studying the distant silhouette of Seattle.

"Where every prospect pleases, and only man is vile," he chanted.

"Shut up, Cappy," his cousin chided him. "Father wants to sleep. Don't you, father?"

Mr. Fridley responded with a protracted mock snore.

*

The next morning I worked, helping Steve hang new nets and paint fresh service stripes on a couple of courts. When I got back to the clubhouse there was a note waiting for me:

Lunch at the Fridleys today one-ish.
I'll pick you up otherwise certain
you'll get lost.

It was signed with a squiggle which could have been any letter in the alphabet.

I showed it to Steve who shook his head dolefully. "Mucho careful," he warned. "The Fridleys grind up dudes like you for taco chips."

"Are they rich?"

"Rich and reckless. Take care."

"You needn't worry. I don't find her attractive."

"Omigawd!" he said with simulated horror. "There goes another one down the tubes! Just remember, dude, when you're drowning in six feet of sweat, don't call me, I ain't the fire department."

*

She picked me up in a tangerine Porsche 914 two-seater, a car which is built to be driven fast, and she certainly answered its challenge. After five exciting minutes down the road toward the Seattle ferry she turned off on a narrow strip of asphalt through heavy forest. A mile into the woods she skidded to a stop alongside a rustic drinking trough.

"How is it?" she abruptly asked.

"How is what?"

"The poison oak."

"I thought we weren't going to talk about it."

"That was yesterday." She critically examined the rash on my neck. "Roll up your sleeve." I did so and she took a long hard look at the sores on my arm. "They're beginning to crust along the edges. That's a good sign."

"It is?"

"Yes. It's past the primary stage now. Come on. Time for a drink of water."

I did as she commanded and we gulped alternately from the mossy old trough.

"Pure," she said. "It's spring fed. Absolutely uncontaminated."

I agreed; as I knelt for another mouthful of the cold, fresh water I saw her poking about in the underbrush.

"What are you looking for? Mushrooms?"

"I'm looking for the villain." And then in a moment, triumphantly, "Here he is! *Rhus diversiloba* himself." She held up a handful of glossy green leaves which she had stripped from a shrub. "Don't touch them. Don't even come close. It's poison oak."

THE RACQUET   33

I was alarmed. "Won't you catch it?"

She stood there, a triumphant wood-goddess, her long yellow hair dappled with sunlight. "I'm immune," she declared. "Absolutely immune. Ten per cent of all people are. I could roll around in it naked and I wouldn't get it. It's what you eat and how you exercise. And your metabolism and your immune system. And then I guess I was born lucky."

She arranged the leaves in a neat rosette around the base of the fountain, an offering to nature from one of her uniquely gifted daughters. I eyed the ring of bright venomous foliage now collecting splash-drops of clear water and reflected on the difficulties of belonging to the ninety per cent who were born not so lucky.

"Let's go," she said softly after a minute-long, contemplative, almost reverential, silence. "You must be starved."

PURIFICATION

The Fridleys' house was set on a knoll surrounded by several hectares of cleared pasture. Here and there were giant oaks and madroña trees. The house itself was grand without being really overbearing about it, perhaps because it was built of weathered wood and each wing just seemed to happen without the intervention of an architect. Anyway, I didn't feel uncomfortable entering it in my none-too-clean tennis whites as I would have in any house that size in South America. Another good omen was that the gray-haired butler, whom Sabrina called Milo, went about his duties in blue jeans. All the same the shadow of money—lots and lots of it—was everywhere.

We ate lunch from a Philippine mahogany table the size of a squash court. There were four of us—the cousin, who seemed to be a semi-permanent attachment to the household; Vicki, a thirtyish friend with migraines and an impending divorce; Sabrina, and I. "Father sends his regrets," Sabrina explained. "He took the early ferry to Seattle. I think he's having lunch with his mistress."

"She's not what you think," Vicki said gaily. "When he pretends to be out catting around he's usually at the public library doing research. I've caught him there myself—you can't imagine how mortified the poor old darling was at being found out." Vicki had scarlet lips and wore lots of rouge and heavy violet eyeshadow and kohl lining her lower lids. Like a *puta*, I thought, why does she paint herself like that? And without thinking my gaze went from her to Sabrina who would never under any circumstances be mistaken for one.

"All the Fridleys have been cerebral Don Juans," the cousin said. And, rolling his eyes, "Present company always excepted."

"Milo, you may bring in the steamed clams," Sabrina said. "Milo dug them himself this morning at daybreak. Didn't you, Milo?"

"Yes, miss." Milo passed around a silver bucket of clams. "At Butcher's Cove just at low tide. In my rubber boots." Both he and his wife Nelly who popped in from the kitchen to chat now and then, spoke with a peculiar rolling accent which I assumed was Scottish.

The clams were preceded by a hot barley broth and followed by a tomato aspic.

"Rob has been hideous about the settlement," Vicki announced. "When I left the lawyer's I had an unbearably beastly headache, but fifteen minutes with that sweet Dr. Yuen and I was perfectly all right. The first three needles did it, darling—just above the knee, on the instep, and in the fleshy pad below the metatarsus. What bliss!"

"I don't think I'd care for that," the cousin said. "God didn't frame me to be a pincushion."

"But you don't feel it at all," Vicki protested. "Only the relief, the sheer bliss of the relief."

"All the same my objection stands."

"Ask Milo," Vicki said. "He can give a proper testimonial. Milo!"

"Yes, ma'am?"

"How did acupuncture work for you?"

"Acupuncture?" He rolled the word around in his mouth as if he were testing a dubious clam.

"Yes, the needles," Vicki persisted. "The time Dr. Kains put the needles in your shoulder."

Milo struggled to recall. "Well, yes, ma'am, we did observe some improvement in our hearing, didn't we?"

Then after a pause he added, "For a time, for a time," and went on gathering up the empty clamshells.

Lunch over, Sabrina announced, "I'm going to show Agosto the house." Vicki and the cousin discreetly retreated and we set off through the ground-floor rooms. They were large and ill-heated but otherwise pretty impressive. But there were Indian masks mounted on all the walls, which I found a bit frightening. "It's as if they're watching us," I said, "and don't much like what they see."

"No," Sabrina answered, "they're old friends, just a bit grumpy today." We stopped before an oak door carved with seraphim. "Father's library and work room. We can't go in without an invitation. But you can look." Through the half-opened door I saw bookshelves to the rafters, piles of old magazines and, incongruously, a formica-enclosed computer work station. "Father is a scholar." From her tone she might have been saying, "Father is an archbishop." Then, less reverentially, "He's also a banker, but that's only to protect us against inflation."

Next came the kitchen where she stopped to talk with Nelly, but the cook's accent had even more oatmeal in it than her husband's and I got only one word out of three. From here we stepped outside and walked the vegetable and flower gardens. There were two men at work in the shrubs; I almost expected them to doff their caps and stand at attention while she passed, but they ignored us and went on spading.

She gave me a mischievous smile. "Cappy thinks you are very handsome. You'd better watch out."

"Your cousin is interested in men?" The possibility hadn't occurred to me.

"Oh, he's *interested* in everything. Maybe even sheep. But it's all theoretical. I think he's a complete virgin. Imagine—at twenty-eight! Shall we go see the horses?

They're probably starving for affection. Dr. Kains says Cappy is the archetype of the masturbatory loner. But of course he's very sensitive and knows an incredible amount about the Eighteenth Century."

"Who is Dr. Kains?"

"My mother's dermatologist."

"And your mother? She's not here?"

"No. She went away to be a countess. She always hankered after that lifestyle and when the chance came she jumped at it. I think she's in Rome now—her husband is only a *Papal* count and she had to convert to get that, but I guess it's what she wanted. Poor father! He couldn't quite keep up."

"It must be sad for him."

"It is. Anyway, I sort of inherited Dr. Kains."

"And you, Sabrina Fridley, with a skin like the inside of a rose petal, require the services of a dermatologist?"

"That's very nicely put, Agosto."

"I thought you didn't like bullshit."

"There are times when it is more acceptable than others."

"And this is one of those times?"

"It could be. Actually, I rather enjoy it. As long as *you* know that *I* know that that's what it is. Does that make any sense?"

"Perfect sense. I'll keep it in mind."

"Do. Of course, he's also an allergist."

"And what does he treat you for?"

"Well, he knows everything there is to know about pollen."

"Pollen?"

"Yes, pollen. And air pollutants, too. He's a professor at the University. You have to meet him."

"If you command it," I said with a mock bow.

"I don't. But I think you'll like him. Here are the

horses. You can try your Latin charm on them." We had reached the stables; Nelly had given her a bag of carrots and now she gave some to me. The horses whinnied in delight and stamped on their stall floors. We fed them for a few moments until the proximity of all that eager, vibrant animal flesh began to affect me. I put an arm around Sabrina's waist and—I should like to say 'swept her up in my arms' but that wasn't quite it—pulled her close to me. For a sweet but all too brief moment she yielded and returned my pressure, but then gently removed my hand.

"We've got to get you well first."

I said I was perfectly well where it counted.

"I'm sure you are." She laughed. "You're a very attractive male, Agosto."

"Thank you."

"And quite sexy. Particularly when you're not trying too hard."

"That rates half a thank-you."

"I should tell you though, Agosto—" here she turned sober and un-playful—"that with me there has to be something else without which I just don't get off the ground."

"And that is—?"

"Well . . . call it psychic affinity. That has to be there. Oh, sex is lovely, don't get me wrong, but without that . . . that . . . ." She broke down in mid-sentence; we hung there together, Sabrina and I, groping for the ineffable essence which was to make us whole.

"And between us . . . it isn't there?" I said at last.

"I don't know, I just don't know." She almost wailed. "This is all so new. So recent. We have to be patient. Perhaps it will come, but we can't force it. Either it will be there or it won't, in its own good time."

We turned into the orchard; there the apple trees, unconcerned with psychic affinities, had burst into full bloom. I felt that the next step was up to me; it was my turn to be honest.

"I'll tell the truth, Sabrina."

"Oh do!"

"I don't know if I even like you."

She took my hand warmly and fixed her gorgeous deep-blue eyes on my face. I think she was beginning to see I had a soul.

"Good!" she said with enthusiasm. "You're being honest at last!"

"But what's horrible is that I think I'm falling in love with you."

"Oh, no, no!"

"Yes," I said sadly. "I think so."

"I meant, no, no, don't do it. Put a stop to it before it gets out of hand."

"It isn't that easy."

"I know it isn't. But make the effort. Without any real affinity it will be an utter disaster. Believe me, Agosto, I *know*. I've been down that road before." She paused, whirled once or twice around the trunk of an apple tree, and seemed to be watching the petals fall. Then she asked, "What is it you don't like about me?"

"Specifically?"

"Yes. Specifically."

"I'm not sure I can remember the details."

"That's absolute bullshit, Agosto. You've lots of things on your mind or you wouldn't have said what you did. Unless you only did it to provoke me, and that would be unforgivably dishonest."

She had me pinned to the wall there, so I began listing all her traits which disturbed me—her intellectual arrogance, her cataloguing mind, the way she asked questions as if she were in a courtroom, her slightly dirty fingernails, her perpetual restlessness, her gaze which some people would consider an impolite stare, her overly methodical forehand returns, her bluntness, her unpredictable anguishes, her—the list went on and on, some of it real, some just inspired by the artist in me. But she listened to it all, sense and nonsense alike, and when, exhausted, I finally stopped, she said cheerfully, "I have a wonderful idea, Agosto."

"Yes?"

"On Monday Vicki and I are going in for a purification run-down. Come join us. It won't cost you a cent. Dr. Kains is doing it out of love."

"But what is it?"

"You'll see. There's a wind-up and a run-down. This is the run-down. It gets rid of all the toxins that have been building up in our bodies. Purification opens up your pores. It frees you. Five hours in the sauna every day. Oh, not steadily—lots of cold showers in between. But you really sweat."

"I do that on the tennis court."

"This is different. You'll see."

My mind was an utter fog. But there was one overriding image in it, an image which rendered me helpless to resist: I saw Sabrina, compactly tucked into a leopard-skin bikini, seated alongside me in a sauna for five hours each and every day.

"Whatever it is," I said. "I'll give it a try."

"It's really a liberation trip." And, taking my hands in hers, she drew me toward her for an unliberated, sisterly kiss. There were apple blossoms tangled in her yellow, disorderly hair. Then she laughed and broke away.

"You know, as you were talking I recognized all the things my mother used to say to me." We began to jog back toward the big house. "Before she became a countess, of course. Afterwards she wasn't so critical."

MAN OF ACTION

So began the most stupefying three days of my life. Let me say first that I've always admired the Finnish people and I respect their invention. I can see its value after a day of wood-chopping or reindeer-hunting in the icy forests of Lapland. And the grizzled hunter leaping from the dry heat straight into a snowbank is truly *macho*. But in South America nature provides us with plenty of heat, both wet and dry, and getting the sweat glands going is never much of a problem. So saunas are unknown—and unnecessary—except in posh hotels and Andean ski clubs that want to entice the tourist with a touch of Old Europe. In Japan I had been in baths with some of the sauna's features, even the hot stones for producing instant steam, but there my time was short and the novelty of the experience protected me from its essential horrors.

First of these horrors was the discovery that the Bainbridge Spa and Tennis Club kept males and females strictly segregated, which effectively took all the bounce out of my treatment. Instead, a dozen of us—ten women and two men—gathered at the juice bar in early afternoon for tofu and guidance—this last dispensed by a señora called the *retreat counsellor*—and then retired to our dressing rooms to commence the day's programmed sweat. This involved alternating fifteen minutes in the sauna with five minutes under the needles of a cold shower. We kept this up for five straight hours, hours of hell which only some existential poet could have thought up. There were amenities, of course. Every hour or so the retreat counsellor sent us vitamins, salt tablets and concoctions of seaweed and fish oil so that our metabolisms wouldn't be utterly destroyed. And then at five-thirty we were allowed to gather, fully clothed, male and female alike, and re-hash our 'experiences' on the hard road to purification. But by then I was too completely enervated to enjoy anything.

The inside of our torture box was of cedar. There was one small window high up in the door, designed so that a passing jailor could inspect the convicts, a round thermometer, a small pan of water, and an enclosed heap of juvenile boulders to throw it on. That was all. The view was considerably less interesting than a jumbled TV screen, and watching a dryer in a laundromat was sheer melodrama by comparison. Indeed, I often imagined that dryer: now a coarse bath towel on top, now the sleeves of a supplicating shirt; next a shriveled sock leaping astride a pair of zebra-striped shorts—everything jumbled, contending for place, striving for notice; but there in our sauna was nothing, only four monotonous walls built of cedar boards carefully chosen for their monotony—free of knots, pitch-pockets, insect holes, seams or any other feature worth looking at. In that sauna even the lumber was totally blah.

My partner in the run-down was a flabby youth named Wesley who was trying to drop ten kilos in a hurry so that he could pass the firemen's exam. He wasn't interested in purification, only weight loss. On our first day together he eyed my poison oak rash with suspicion—it certainly wasn't getting any better in the heat—and moved to the far, non-leprous, end of the sauna. Occasionally a racquetball player or two would join us in the box, but generally we were alone, Wesley and I, watching our life forces !each away. And if Wesley wouldn't talk at least I got to know his body

in far more detail than I ever did my own brother's—
every crease, fold, pimple and follicle on his belly and
buttocks, the unruly black curl at the nape of his neck,
the bald spot, the bloodshot gray-green eyes, the small,
reclusive, manicured penis—for what else was there
to look at?

But although I hadn't foreseen it, relief was on its
way. On the third day of this torture we were visited
by Dr. Kains, the allergist who was nominally in charge
of purifying us. He was a trim, forceful man of about
fifty who spoke with a slight European accent. He had
tightly curled black hair and large glistening teeth just
a little too regular to be his own. All the same, I liked
him right away; he exuded professional competence.
When it came time to interview me he saw immediately that something was wrong.

"You shouldn't be in there for five hours with that
dermatitis," he said. "Just a normal fifteen minutes a
day will be plenty." He consulted his chart and read
my name aloud. "Who recommended this treatment
for you?" he asked in good Spanish.

"No one," I answered. "I volunteered." I certainly
didn't plan to get Sabrina in trouble.

"Well, you can un-volunteer. It isn't appropriate.
Besides, you seem to be in fine shape already. Just let
me take a look at that poison oak." He continued talking to me in Spanish; I got the feeling he would have
dealt with Italian, German or Hungarian patients just
as fluently. He gave my rash an inspection and wrote
a prescription for a new medicine. "You're an athlete?"

"A tennis player."

"The active life, that's the answer. Well, apply this stuff
morning and night and we'll have your skin straightened out in no time."

"Thank you, doctor."

"And don't starve yourself—it doesn't pay." With another flash of his ultra-bright teeth he moved on to the waiting Wesley.

"Dr. Kains says you are to be dropped from the program," our squad leader announced when I appeared for the usual five-thirty Exhaustion Seminar. She made it sound as if I were a snivelling deserter being stripped of my epaulets in front of the whole regiment.

"I know. I just came by for my vee-tamins."

"Your what?"

"Vee-tamins? Vitt-ameens?" This word gives me a lot of trouble.

"VYE-tamins!"

"Yes, them," I said making a grab for my allotted pile.

Vicki, of all people, came to my defense. "It isn't Agosto's fault," her cheerful brassy voice rang out. "He has poison oak and the doctor said only a moron would have let him in in the first place."

Everybody burst into laughter except for Wesley who couldn't and the counsellor who wouldn't—she was apoplectic but since she also taught the courses in Stress Management, she didn't dare show it.

"Thank you for sharing your point of view, Vicki," she said with a tight little smile and dismissed us early.

*

"The Eskimo," said Dr. Kains, "in his normal environment is completely free of allergies. There are no dusts and pollens among the ice-floes."

"But isn't acid rain changing that?" Sabrina asked.

"Only marginally if at all. Whatever the effect of sulfides on the ecology they have yet to enter the Eskimo's food chain in sufficient quantities to threaten his immune system."

"We should be glad of that," said Vicki. Now four kilos lighter and divested of all her war paint, she was beginning to look more like a nurse on holiday.

"However, take that same Eskimo out of his skin hut on Baffin Land—"

"Or his igloo."

"—or his igloo—thank you, Sabrina—and place him in a climatically controlled, dust-free room in Vancouver or Seattle and within weeks he will develop allergic reactions to a wide spectrum of aerobes. Not only does he develop these allergies but—and here's the significant datum—his immune system begins appreciable alterations to protect and, in some cases anticipate, the new threats to his organic stability."

"It seems cruel to bring him all that way just to infect him," Sabrina objected.

Dr. Kains gently set her fears to rest. "He considers it a small price to pay for an all-expenses trip to a world he has hitherto only seen on television. There are far more applicants than we can possibly take."

We had finished our dinner of charbroiled halibut, broccoli, and butterless new potatoes at The Clam Bucket, a restaurant which normally overlooked a broad stretch of the Sound; tonight it was raining and on the deck outside our picture window the Cinzano umbrellas stood with folded dripping wings like storm-bound pelicans.

"A new world for a few sneezes," said Vicki eyeing the forbidden wine bottle by the doctor's glass. "I think I'd go for it, too."

Weary from three hours of racquetball with Steve, I was only half listening. Besides, I had made a discovery which engrossed me: the tangled black curls which framed the doctor's tanned aristocratic face were as false as his teeth; he was wearing a wig, unquestionably a very expensive one but a wig all the same. Why this shocked me I didn't know, but it did. And greater surprises lay ahead.

"I've had to give up rock climbs," Dr. Kains was saying when I next tuned in. "It's too bad—I loved the sport. But I can't get a proper grip on the faces any more."

"Why not?" I asked.

"Show him," Sabrina said to the doctor.

He scuffed off his oxfords and extended his stockinged feet; one was three inches shorter than the other.

"No toes on the left foot," he said casually.

"Did you lose them climbing?"

"No, frostbite. On the Coppermine River. We tried to make it downstream to the Arctic Ocean in an eighteen-foot whaleboat before the river froze up. We were just a week too late. The boat got ice-bound and we had to walk out. Eighty miles of tundra. My left toes didn't make it."

We were rapt. Even the waiter paused in clearing away our dishes. And yet the doctor didn't decorate his story or try to dramatize it, and he didn't take his sock off as a showman surely would have. No, it was all simple and unadorned as if he had been recounting a trip to the corner market.

"When you make a mistake up there," he concluded, "the Arctic doesn't easily forgive you." He put his shoes back on, wincing almost imperceptibly at the left one; either the memory or the flesh itself still hurt. We said nothing more. The rain outside continued its remorseless descent.

"A wonderful man!" Vicki said after he had left to catch the last ferry to Seattle.

"He is that," Sabrina said, "but also a little sinister. What do you think, Agosto?"

"He has had many adventures," I answered. "Perhaps he is a tiny bit worn."

"He wants us to fly with him to the other side of the mountains next week."

"You and Vicki?"

"And you too, Agosto. He likes you. The four of us would go in his plane. It would be a voyage of exploration. Of ourselves and the balance between us, I think he means. Only I'm not sure I'm ready. Purification has done a lot for me, but distances like that still frighten me."

"I'll certainly go if he asks me," I said. "I'm here to see America."

"Yes," Sabrina said reflectively. "For you it would be easy. You can be just a tourist when you want to be. You don't have so much at risk."

"Let's go for it, Sabrina," Vicki said enthusiastically. "It'll be a blast. He visits Indians and far-out *rancheros*. He's got people collecting pollen for him all over. You'll love it. Besides, the plane has a built-in bar." Obviously she had flown with Dr. Kains before.

"You can't drink," Sabrina said reproachfully. "Not for thirty days—you promised."

"There's always diet Cola," Vicki said with a pout.

"You're afraid of flying?" I asked Sabrina as I helped her on with her raincoat.

"It's not that. I'm just a little afraid of what I might discover."

"In you?"

"In me. Myself. And I."

She gave me an affectionate yet ethereal smile and we left it like that—perhaps we would go with Dr. Kains, perhaps we wouldn't.

FAMILY AFFAIRS

I was invited again to the big house. This time Mr. Fridley was there and after Milo had cleared away the salad (they ate it last, in the French manner) he asked me into his library. I realized that this was an honor but I knew too that it was a trial and probably a dangerous one. Yet surrounded by his papers and shelves loaded with early legal records, he seemed open and almost jovial. He showed me his master work, a book the size of an unabridged dictionary:

Pioneer Families
of
King County
Washington
by
Samuel F. B. Fridley, M.A., B.Litt. Oxon.
General Editor, Early Settlers
Editions
Seattle, 1986

It was impressive and I told him so. He entered a modest disclaimer. "Of course, my cousin Caspar Fridley, whom you have met, helped in the compilation. But both senior and junior branches of the Fridley family were my responsibility, as well as the Hendersons and Frothinghams and the monograph on pioneer tavern signs. The introduction is by our friend Professor Laszlo Kains . . . No, Caspar isn't on the title page—he prefers the cloak of anonymity."

We turned to the computer with its neatly arrayed files of tapes and disks. "On these floppies—what a neologism that is!—we have every last soul on the King County tax rolls and public records—marriages, births,

deaths, mortgages, that sort of thing—from the year 1832, when the first District Clerk began keeping them, until 1914. That's our cut-off date." He sighed. "The First World War, you know. The beginning of the end. Look." He flicked the viewer on, punched a few keys and came up with a steady succession of Fridleys.
"There are certainly a great many of them, sir," I offered.
"One hundred and seventy-three at the latest count." The necrology of the Tribe of Fridley continued whirring past. "But every week or so we turn up a new one. Any other favorites?"
"Favorites?"
"Names."
I suggested we try Villaseñor.
"Not many of them, I'm afraid. The Spanish land grant families didn't make it this far north." However, he dutifully punched the keys and we got:

> Villa, Francisco (Pancho), 1877-1923.
> pseud. of Araungo, Doroteo. Mex.
> revolutionist & bandit. Raided Columbus,
> N.M., August 1916. Many fatalities.

"Of course," Mr. Fridley said, "there's no hard evidence he ever made it to King County but we like to keep well-known period figures on file; you can't tell when fresh data may turn up." He tried the keys again. "Sorry, no Villaseñor. Of course one of them may have worked for the Great Northern laying tracks or in the fish canneries but we don't have the payroll records any more. Vanished. Vanished." He flicked off the viewer. "Utterly vanished. Please sit down, Agosto, you can't be comfortable standing there."

"Thank you, sir." I could see heavy weather coming up over the horizon.

Mr. Fridley took off his glasses and wiped the mist

from them. Like his daughter, his eyes were protuberant; they gave him a slightly froglike stare.

"I want to ask you a question, Agosto," he said after a sizable silence.

I told him I was ready.

"Do you think I am wasting my life on all this? Be honest. Is it a waste of time and talent?"

"Not in the least, sir." I was glad of the opening he offered. "There is nothing more important than the family. And if we don't have a sense of its historical continuity, how can it possibly survive?"

"You're not just being polite?"

"Mr. Fridley sir—"

"Samuel. My name is Samuel. You may call me Samuel just as I call you Agosto."

"Thank you, Mr. Samuel. What I wanted to say is that I have been brought up in a culture where family traditions are cherished. We have a proverb in Spanish that goes, the single tree draws the lightning, the forest laughs at it."

"That's very well put."

I could see that I was cheering him up so I charged right ahead: "I can think of nothing more important, sir, than keeping the flame of family tradition alight—so that even in the darkest of nights it will be a beacon for the younger generation."

"You believe that?"

"With all my heart."

He considered that in silence, and then he said in a casual—perhaps too casual—voice, "Sabrina tells me you are a brilliant tennis player."

"She exaggerates, sir," I said modestly.

"Yes, she does that occasionally," Mr. Fridley observed. "But you are ranked, I believe?"

"Only Number 224."

"But to have attained international ranking at your age, Agosto, is quite an achievement. Don't sell yourself short." He saw my puzzled look and added, "—a phrase from the stock exchange, a neologism, I fear, one of the many which are corrupting the English tongue."

Outside the library window, which overlooked the Sound, I saw the English language fly by in tatters.

"Sabrina says your family is in the restaurant industry." I saw he was getting down to business at last.

"That must be very exciting these days."

I love my father and am proud of him. "My father works for Hyatt Hotels. For twenty years he has worked for the Hyatts. He is a waiter, first-class, in their dining room."

I could see him stiffen but he was a good sport and never lost control. "I waited tables myself," he said with an urbane smile, "when I was an undergraduate at Stanford."

"With my father it is a profession, an art form. He is entrusted with preparing *biftek Diane* and *crêpes Suzette*, for example. They have to be cooked on a brazier at the tableside—one mistake and everything is ruined. This year he is first in line to become a wine steward."

"Yes, yes," said Mr. Fridley. "There is a distinction, I would be the first to recognize it. To tell the truth, I wasn't very good at the . . . profession. In point of fact, my first day was very nearly my last; I upset a tray and spilled iced tea all over the Dean of Women."

We jointly smiled at the remembered awkwardness. Mr. Fridley cleared his throat. "And your father continues to follow his profession in Montevideo?"

"Not in Montevideo. In Mexico City."

"I see. I see." But it was plain he didn't. There was a pause during which he obviously weighed, balanced, and rejected what he, no doubt, would call 'verbal alternatives.' Then he tried again. "Somewhere, I think, Sabrina intimated, or at least dropped a hint, that you were of Uruguayan nationality."

"I have an Uruguayan passport, Samuel. But I am Mexican by birth."

"Yes," he said affably. "Mexico. A great people, a great culture."

But I knew instantly that he didn't mean it.

I've noticed that North Americans react to Latinos in inverse proportion to the distance between them. If you come from a place very far away which can only be visited by an expensive flight or a cruise-ship equipped with plenty of Greek or Italian waiters, then you're considered 'exotic' and can be invited home for dinner. But the closer you live to the United States the less glamour you have; and there at the very bottom of the totem pole you'll find the Mexican. Many kilometers breed romance; a scarcity of them gives rise to fear and loathing. I saw Mr. Fridley's discomfort, so I hastened to relieve it.

"Both my parents were born in Spain," I said.

"In Spain?" He noticeably brightened.

"Yes, in Andalusia. Near Seville."

"I see. That is in southern Spain?"

"Yes, sir."

"The more Moorish part of the kingdom, if I remember my Lope de Vega aright."

"Yes, sir." I hastened to reassure him. "But *their* parents, my *abuelos*, were from Valladolid, in the North. I think they were just visiting Seville at the time."

"Ah," said Mr. Fridley. "Genealogy is a great study. I'm glad you've kept up with it, Agosto."

I assured him that genealogy was an important and enduring part of my life.

He offered me his hand. "I'm glad we've gotten to know each other better. Please think of my *casa* as *su casa* while you're here on Puget Sound."

I returned his brisk, bony handshake.

"Thank you, Samuel, sir."

"The pleasure is mine, Agosto."

Outside on the porch I ran across Cousin Caspar, his feet up on the railing. The rain had stopped and the night had turned soft. When Cousin Caspar saw me coming he waved his cigar and chanted:

> "Sabrina fair,
> Goddess of the silver lake
> Listen for dear honor's sake,
>   Listen and save!"

"That's very beautiful," I said.

He seemed a bit drunk. "It's Milton. From *Comus*, I think. Which is all about chastity and wanting what you won't ever get."

I said I was not familiar with British literature; now if he had quoted from Cervantes . . .

"But that will be Rosina, not Sabrina. Those girls only have the rhyme in common."

"I've always admired Don Quixote," I went on, "for his persistence in spite of all difficulties. Admired and, I hope, learned from him."

"Indeed?" he said with a tipsy grin. "I should have thought Sancho Panza was more your role model."

I knew that he was trying to insult me but I discovered long ago that the best way to parry insults is with a mask of innocence. "I admire Sancho Panza, too," I said. "He was very Spanish."

"You admire everyone, don't you?"

I saw no point in an overhead smash when I could put him away with a drop shot: "Wasn't it one of your poets who said that love is what makes the world go 'round?"

He ground out what was left of his cigar in the potted juniper and said in a purring voice, "I wish I could believe you were as fatuous as that sounds, but I don't."

"Thank you for sharing," I said sweetly and went off to find Sabrina.

She had to drive me home, of course. We got into the Porsche and under the pretense of helping tie her scarf I nibbled at her ear. "Don't!" she said fretfully and lashed the car down the drive. She was upset, but fortunately it was with her father, not with me.

"He grilled you?"

"He asked me a few questions."

"It's totally humiliating. He does his District Attorney gig with every single male who enters the house. It's simply ghastly."

I said that I had rather enjoyed the clash of wits.

"Perhaps *you* do," she retorted. "But it humiliates *me*. And that's just what he intends by it, to humiliate me. It's only morbid curiosity on his part, he can't *do* a thing. As the heavy father he's absolutely, totally ineffectual. I'm going to do just what I want and he knows it perfectly well. But he can't resist playing that role. He's an utter worm."

"But he was really very friendly."

"Don't defend him," she said imperiously. "That's just his cunning and deceit. He doesn't mean a word of it."

Since that too was basically my opinion, I said nothing more. The car plunged through the sinuous dark and we each sank into our own night-thoughts. When we entered the village she brightened.

"Thank God he isn't coming on Saturday. I couldn't bear that."

I caught at the implication. "Then you *are* going to

come with Dr. Kains?"

"Yes. I think so."

"I'm very happy to hear it."

"I think I'm changing, Agosto. Since I finished the purification run-down. I felt something snap the last day and a lot of little impurities, a lot of my hesitations and reservations disappear . . . "

"You look beautiful," I said, and meant it. The days in the sauna had given her skin an amazing glow.

"Don't say that! I don't want to be beautiful. Everyone's always saying that, and what they mean is that they don't respect your mind." She looked at me critically. "It's too bad you couldn't complete the course, Agosto."

"You know why."

"Yes, I know why. It wasn't your fault. Still, I wish you had. You would see things with a different aureole around them."

Slightly uncomfortable with aureoles, I changed the subject.

"How far are we going to fly?"

"I don't know. To somewhere in Eastern Oregon. Laszlo has his little pollen-collectors all over and he won't tell you where until he's ready to take off. Are you excited?"

"Very. And you?"

"I love volcanoes," she answered. "We're going to fly over three of them. Won't that be wonderful?"

"Yes," I said. "It's all going to be wonderful."

Now that her anger had passed she had turned warm and affectionate. She stopped the Porsche in front of my place, turned off the lights and gave me a lingering goodnight kiss. She no longer kept her body away from mine; I could feel that her reserve was beginning to melt.

"Until Saturday, then."

We kissed again, even more fervently.

"Watch out," she said with a laugh. "You're getting me tangled in the gear-shift."

"Good night."

"Good night."

The Porsche disappeared down the coast road. Whether or not it was the thought of volcanoes and flying that excited her, I was making progress; at least there were no more references to poison oak.

WEEKENDING IN OREGON

I was at the Winslow airstrip promptly at seven Saturday morning. Dr. Kains was ahead of me, affable and trim in his nylon flight jacket and pilot's cap. He had already checked the engine and done his preflight testing. He showed me around his plane, a Comanche; he was obviously proud of it. Then we had coffee with the on-duty mechanic at the hangar and waited for the ladies. They hadn't shown up by seven-thirty and the doctor grew increasingly irritated.

"I should have guessed it," he said. "They've gone on strike."

"If you like, sir," I offered, "I could phone Sabrina and see if she has left yet."

"It won't do any good. She spent the night in town with Vicki so they could get an early start."

We paced restlessly around the tarmac for another fifteen minutes, then he exploded, "Silly cunts! They don't care how they waste your time." I had never heard Dr. Kains use offensive language before; he saw my surprise and offered an explanation: "Excuse the outburst. It's entirely my fault. I had a row with Vicki last night and now they're both punishing me for it."

No doubt it was obtuse of me but this was the first suspicion I'd had of an affair between them. Not that I ought to have been surprised—Vicki was obviously ready for anything and Dr. Kains was an attractive if slightly mature man. But I did find it bad luck that Sabrina and I should be caught up in their quarrel. I certainly never had the least idea that (as Vicki later told me) it was Sabrina herself who was behind their non-arrival.

"Well, I have to fly," the doctor said at last. "I've

got an appointment in The Dalles this afternoon and I'm late already. You can wait for them if you want, Agosto, but it should be a lovely clear day to view the Cascades."

A weekend without Sabrina was certainly not what I had been anticipating, but I swallowed my disappointment. *"No hay problema,"* I said cheerfully. *"Vamonos."* And got in my seat and buckled up.

We flew south and east. First over Puget Sound and the city of Seattle, then as we gained altitude we skirted the snowy mass of Mount Rainier, a peak I thought even more beautiful than Fuji. I enjoyed the flight greatly. It was noisy enough that conversation was difficult but that was all right with me, and the scenery was magnificent. There is a big difference between flying commercially at nearly ten thousand meters where everything is flattened out beneath you and at two or three thousand meters where you actually seem to be threading your way between the great snow-covered crags. You become one with the land, you share its dangers and rewards. And always beneath us we could clearly see our ghost-brother, our plane's shadow, coursing over the rocks and mountain valleys. South of Rainier Dr. Kains pointed out the vast scar in the land which had been Mount Saint Helens, the scene of the greatest of recent North American volcanic explosions. He circled the raw crater, now softened a bit by a fresh snowfall, and then turned south. In another hour we passed Mount Adams and then picked up Mount Hood and the Columbia River winding beneath us, followed it upstream for a while, and came down on a rather pitted and bumpy airstrip.

"The Dalles," he announced. "You're in Oregon."

The country seemed dry and dusty although it was

THE RACQUET

still not full summer. It reminded me a bit of parts of the Brazilian uplands.

We got out to stretch. "There's a phone here some place," Dr. Kains said. "I'm going to call the girls and see what happened to them. Watch the plane."

He had been gone five minutes when a very dusty pickup truck drove out on the tarmac and stopped alongside our plane. The driver got out and sauntered over. He was dressed in a tan whipcord leisure suit and wore lizard-skin boots, a large chestnut-colored moustache and a green-visored cap with the name *John Deere* on it. He seemed very friendly.

"Is the good doctor in, buddy?" he asked.

I explained that he had gone to make a call.

"Ain't exactly office hours, eh?" He consulted his watch. "Tell him I'll be back at half past."

"Who shall I say called?" I asked, trying to be helpful.

"He'll know." And he got back in his pickup and drove off.

When Dr. Kains returned I told him that a man from the tractor company had been there. "Yes," he laughed, "it's one of my collectors. He's been gathering ragweed samples."

I asked him if he had reached the ladies. He looked distracted. Yes, he had gotten through. "They send you their regrets. Vicki has one of her migraines; Sabrina felt she had to take care of her." He took out his wallet and gave me a $100 bill. "There's a motel just down the road. Go get us a room, we're going to overnight here. You'd better sign my name so I can find it when I get back."

"And then?"

"Just wait for me in the room. Don't go out, just wait. I'll be along soon. I'll tell you all about it when I get there."

There was mystery here but I didn't think to question him—in Uruguay a professor, a *catedrático*, sits on the right hand of God and you do as he tells you. So I walked to the motel, checked us in and lay on the bed watching a re-run of *Black Beauty*. In about an hour Dr. Kains came in carrying an apple box with four bulging paper bags in it.

"Sorry to disturb you," he said politely. "But you had better get your things. I hope you haven't unpacked."

"We're not staying?"

"No. We are revising our schedule."

I flicked off the TV. "I might be able to get the room-rent back. Or at least part of it. The beds haven't even been turned back."

"Let's be generous," he said with a munificent smile. "It was money well spent. Now help me carry the box, will you, Agosto? It's getting heavy."

"I hope it's what you need for your experiments."

"*Absolutamente,*" he said. "It's excellent pollen. From four different locales."

He had a taxi waiting outside. We drove to the airstrip; when we came alongside he over-tipped the driver and we jumped into the plane again.

"Buckle up," he commanded. "We'll overnight in Klamath Falls and then fly back by way of Astoria and the coast."

But I wasn't destined for Klamath Falls, not that trip. We hadn't been in the air more than ten minutes when, with no warning, the engine coughed once or twice and then failed.

"Shit!" said Dr. Kains. "She's out of gas."

I looked at the gauge. It was on empty.

"We're on empty," I said inanely.

Dr. Kains ground his dentures. With the engine silent that sound took on monstrous proportions, like the growl of a lion in a remote cave.

"Those fucking cowboys!" he swore. "One of them drained the tank."

"But why would they want to do that?"

He glared at me, a glare which seemed to contain all earthly hatred mingled with scorn for my stupidity—but it was only for an instant, then the plane demanded his attention. He ground his horsy teeth again and shouted, "Hold your balls, man, we're going down!" And almost instantly the gray ghosts of sagebrush began whizzing past the windows. There was a dirt road just ahead and he made for it, only to come up twenty meters short in a patch of dark green junipers. The plane emitted a crackling screech as it tore off half a dozen treetops, then scrunched to a sickening stop which threw me so hard against my seatbelts that I thought my ribs would break, and at last tipped over gently until one wing-tip rested in a juniper bush. In a second I had unbuckled and dropped from the plane amazed to find my bones still worked. As my feet hit the ground I began running and didn't stop until I was a hundred meters off—naturally, I expected an explosion and fire, but when I turned around to look the Comanche lay there gleaming in its red-and-white paint, looking almost undamaged in the midday sunlight. I laughed in relief—we were out of gas so there was nothing much to burn. Cautiously I went back and crawled into the cockpit to see how the doctor had fared.

Not too well, I'm afraid. He sat slumped over the wheel, both lenses of his glasses splintered, his curly toupee hanging from one ear by a bit of collodion. For the first time I saw how bald he really was, like an Easter egg and a cracked one at that. There was blood on the windshield and more on his forehead. For a second I thought he was one of those mannequins they use in test crashes. It was obvious what had happened:

he had ordered me to buckle up but in his haste had omitted fastening his own unwieldy shoulder-belt. I tried to find his pulse but there was none. It was a case of instant skull fracture. As Sabrina would have put it, he was absolutely totally dead.

At this point my instinct for self-preservation took over. I cut a hole in one of the paper bags the doctor had picked up in The Dalles. A yellow powder trickled out; I tasted it; it was pollen all right but what kind of pollen and from what kind of plant I couldn't tell. Perhaps it was saffron; perhaps sun-flower. However, I am well aware that some pollens are more legal than others and I certainly didn't plan to be there when they tested it. So I filled a canteen with Pepsi-Cola, took a few tuna-fish and beansprout sandwiches from the fridge and, after wiping my fingerprints off all door handles, I dropped down into the desert and began walking. Fast. *Adios, Dr. Kains,* I said to myself, *sayonara.* I was genuinely sorry about the way things had turned out for him. He had been so friendly and generous, it was a shame he came to such an abrupt end but now I had my own welfare to consider.

Half a kilometer away I stopped and looked back. I could still see the plane, a beautiful fallen aluminum leaf gleaming in the gray sea of sagebrush.

URIM AND THUMMIM

That night I slept in a stack of new-mown alfalfa and ate the last of the health-food sandwiches Vicki had fixed for her late lover. Fortunately the evening was warm and my improvised bed fragrant and soft. I awoke to blazing sunlight and a circle of cows staring at me with contemplative semi-interest. I stared back, wishing I knew some way to milk them since I had no other prospects for breakfast. I calculated that I had walked twenty kilometers from the scene of the wreck and my feet, shod in my one pair of dress shoes, were already blistered. Luckily I was picked up by the driver of Purina Chow's feed truck. His name was Floyce Bellew (I still have his business card) and he offered to take me to Bend, Oregon, half way to California, if I would help him with a few ranch deliveries on the way. Naturally, I accepted his kind offer.

We made a couple of minor stops where I bucked sacks of hen-scratch into the barns while Mr. Bellew tried to smooth-talk the farmers into buying patented feeders, then we drove into the ranch home of Pinchot Kennels, our big customer of the day. Here we were greeted by a full-throated chorus from some forty-five hounds taking their daily exercise in fenced dog-runs. "Biggest hound-dog ranch in Central Oregon," Mr. Bellew informed me.

There were five dozen sacks of kibble to unload and Mr. Bellew showed me how to stack and wheel them into a storeroom while he demonstrated his feeders to the owner, Mr. Gaylord Pinchot. I saw now why he had stopped his truck for me but even though I had been trapped into it I worked hard at creating the right impression—that's always the best way. When I had finished, Mr. Pinchot, obviously impressed, asked me my name and nationality and then suggested that I break my trip and sign on at Pinchot Kennels for a month or so. "You've got good muscle tone," he observed like a judge at a dog show, "and I see he don't have to tell you twice how to buck dog feed." He was a wispy little man with wet brown eyes and badly shaven jowls, something like a basset-hound himself. People often come to look like their animals if they live close enough to them, and Mr. Pinchot, I was to discover, was closer to no one more than his hounds.

So I accepted his terms and said thank you and goodbye to the Purina Chow man.

"Now we'd better have it out with the old woman," Mr. Pinchot said with grim relish. We entered the house, stopping first to knock the dirt from our shoes on a scraper in the shape of a dachshund. "You wait here. The missus is baking." Mr. Pinchot disappeared into the kitchen while I had a look around the living room. On one wall was a colored lithograph of Jesus carrying his cross up an unbelievably steep hill, beside it a glass case of prize ribbons and rosettes from dog shows; opposite were dozens of brass beagles and bassets, trophies all; on the TV a photo of some stern-looking pioneers in chin-whiskers; and on the oak center table a bowl of wax fruit. Voices were raised in the kitchen, epithets and shouts were exchanged, then after an ominous silence Mrs. Pinchot appeared in the doorway. She was a head taller than her husband and wore her hair piled in a conical bun. Wiping her floury hands on an apron, she looked me over suspiciously and asked:

"Do you believe in a personal God, young man?"

I told her I most definitely did and tried to make it

sincere—the odor of fresh-baked bread floated from the kitchen and I was faint with hunger.

"Do you take whiskey or narcotics?"

"No ma'am, I do not."

"Do you own a motorcycle?"

I denied that, too.

She gave me a dubious look as if she thought me an habitual liar and said to her husband with martyred innocence, "All right, Mister, you hired him so I guess there ain't a thing more I can say."

"I need a hand with the dogs, Mrs. P.," Pinchot said gloomily.

"I heard you, Mister. But remember, young man, no women in your room or out you go. Get it?"

I got it. Luckily the breakfast which now followed was excellent—hotcakes, home-made sausage, new-baked pastries and plenty of coffee—or I would have left that day.

"The old woman is more bark than bite," Mr. Pinchot said as he showed me how to hose down the kennels. "She's got quite a tongue on her, ain't she?" He seemed to take pride in her shrewishness, as if it were one of her show points.

During the time I worked for the Pinchots they regularly fought with one another and when they weren't fighting each needed an audience for grievances. I was that audience.

"The old woman don't give a little red fig for anybody who ain't descended from a Utah pioneer," Mr. P. told me on one occasion.

"Mister Pinchot can't help himself," Mrs. P. informed me on another day. "He's poor white trash and always will be."

At night in the room with the trophies and the wax fruit they usually fell into a sullen truce and let the television talk for them. Naturally I was interested in the TV too—I listened intently for any news of Dr. Kains or his plane crash, but there was nothing. The desert had apparently swallowed him up.

During the days we worked long hours. The work was tiring but I quickly took an interest in it and began to learn about hounds. In Mexico dogs fall into two classes: the spoiled pets of the very rich, or *calleros*–street dogs, scavengers, terrorized and terrorizing, unloved mongrels, ravenous and despised. Pinchot's hounds were from another world—they were work dogs, bold, self-confident in their rabbit-chasing skills, each with a distinct profile.

"Look at this here bitch," said Mr. Pinchot proudly, raising an unprotesting beagle by her ears. "This here is Pinetop Mindy out of Black Friday out of Dune Pillow sired by Max's Sundance, every last one of them double or triple field-champions."

The manhandled dog might yip or squeal but it would never growl or run away. They respected him. He knew by heart the lineage and show points of every animal on the ranch. Where I saw nothing but an undifferentiated mass of open mouths and wagging tails he saw line control, nose for scent, tracking skills. His knowledge continually amazed me. "I ain't much for book learning," he told me. "I make do with the AKC Stud Book on weekdays and the Book of Mormon on Sundays."

On other days he grew nostalgic. "I come from Chubb Hollow, Tennessee," he announced. "And the goldang worst day of my life was the day I left there." Things weren't what they once were. Thirty years ago every Tennessee farmer with a few acres to run them on kept hounds. "Now they all go bowling and skeet-shooting," he said gloomily. "And here in Oregon it's worse.

Ain't no cottontails any more and the jack rabbits have growed such long legs they can outrun almost anything." Another of his villains was the prairie dog. "Them varmints has took over. So goldang many holes in the ground here at Prineville you break your horse's legs if you ride to hounds." The hunters had to walk behind their pack and it was hardly worth the effort. "It ain't a country for the sporting man, Gus, and that's a fact." He kept one pack for sentimental reasons but mainly he hunted with braces, boarded beagles for absent owners, and bred and trained dogs for field shows. There was still some pleasure in that, he admitted.

"Now take this here dog," he said "He's Jimtown Rumpus out of Rusty Gun out of Cherokee Sally, every one a triple champion." He lifted the beagle and went muzzle to muzzle, bristle rubbing bristle. "You're a winner, ain't you?" And Jimtown Rumpus and Mr. P. gazed admiringly into each other's wet brown eyes.

After I had calmed her initial suspicions Mrs. Pinchot took a sort of liking to me. There was an orchard behind the house and one of my chores was to irrigate and care for the fruit trees. It was cherry season and we picked the trees together while Mrs. P. talked to me, sociably, chiefly on religious topics. The Pinchots were tithing members of the Church of Jesus Christ of Latter Day Saints, called the Mormons. This was my first chance to hear their gospel message. Mr. P., she explained, was merely a convert but she herself was connected to many of the first families of Mormonism and knew intimately the history of its martyrs and prophets.

In my childhood I loved my mother's accounts of the magical lives of the saints; now Mrs. P. had a fresh store of miracles for me, certainly no more improbable than the traditional Catholic ones. And she told her stories very well. My favorite concerned a poor young well-digger named Joseph Smith of Palmyra (a magical name!), New York, who was told by a giant angel (here I envisaged a full-bearded eagle) where to dig for a chest (pirate treasure!) full of gold plates (booty of emperors!) on which an entirely new and truthful interpretation of the Holy Bible was inscribed in some seemingly untranslatable language (*Raiders of the Lost Ark*).

Ladder high in my green cherry-bearing sea of leaves, I was seized by an euphoric notion. The name Moroni, of Italian origin, was common in Argentina—it was just possible that the eagle-faced angel Moroni had brought the plates from South America where it was a known fact that the ancient Inca emperors dined off golden platters.

"It's certainly a possibility," admitted Mrs. P.

"In which case," I pursued, "the message to Mr. Smith may well have been written in Quechua."

"Quechua?" She seemed doubtful.

"The language of the ancient Incas."

"I don't think that can be right, Gus. The Book of Mormon says that two other angels came to the Prophet at night and helped him translate the golden plates. The angels were named Urim and Thummim."

"Urim and Thummim!" I came down the ladder with my bucket overflowing with cherries. "Of course! That's Quechua for Courage and Faith. I told you!"

"You speak the language?"

"Only a little," I said glibly. "But I know a lot of the words."

"Imagine that!" Mrs. P. said, giving way to my enthusiasm. "God's Word revealed through the ancient Incas! That would be just one more confirmation of its eternal truth."

"It would indeed," I said. "But I don't think you should set your hopes too high—it's only a theory as yet."

"Just the same, the Incas! Think of that! You could knock me down with a feather." Then a shadow crossed her face and she turned bitter again. "Don't tell the Mister your theory, Gus. He has no head at all for theology. Dogs is all he thinks about."

I agreed it would be better if we kept it to ourselves. But after that there was a special bond between us and I was always served first and with the biggest piece of her cherry pies.

Some Failed Connections

Two weeks passed.

I might have stayed even longer had it not been for an unforeseen complication. The day came when I was to receive my pay, one hundred dollars every two weeks, plus board—those had been the terms.

"You've been a lot of help to me, Gus," Mr. Pinchot said in a fatherly tone. We were in his front room, getting ready for the late-afternoon Farmer's Home program and weather report on the TV.

"Thank you, sir. I've learned a lot."

"Here's what we can spare you just now." He handed me a clean, crisp twenty-dollar bill with a portrait of Gen. Jackson who had thrashed the British at the Battle of New Orleans. "There'll be more next time if some of these dead-beats pay their stud fees on time."

As politely as I could, I reminded him of the sum he had mentioned when I was hired.

"Well, Gus," he said, gazing at me with his liquid brown eyes, "it's true there was some *suggested* figure tossed about between us two, *but* that was before I seen your papers. Now you know and I know, Gus, that you're in this country on a tourist visa; it's stamped there in your passport. And it ain't legal for you to seek or accept employment while on that visa. Furthermore, it ain't legal for Pinchot Kennels to offer you, an undocumented alien, work on any terms whatsoever. That's the law, Gus, and Pinchot Kennels is headed for a pack of trouble if it ignores that law, a pack of trouble."

I said that I could see his difficulty but that I still

thought a promise was a promise, particularly between two Christian men.

"I agree," he said seriously. "That's what I told the old woman—my word's my bond. But she pointed out to me, Gus, that there is likely to be legal expenses involved if we have to defend this case and that it was no more than fair to expect you to bear some of them expenses. So we're setting aside what she calls a *contingency fund* which means money for just in case."

"Just in case . . . ?"

"Just in case the immigration officers was to come out here and ask to see your green card, Gus, that's the just-in-case."

I could see that I was checkmated. There is a proverb in Spanish to the effect that the stubborn oak is broken by the storm, while the pliant willow lives to see the sun again. I chose the way of the willow.

"It's kind of you, sir," I said, "to offer to take care of my legal expenses. I only hope I can justify your faith in me."

He gave me a sort of halfway smile and offered me a cup of Bovril tea. I don't know whether he believed me or not, but it didn't make much difference—he had the upper hand and we both knew it.

That night being a Saturday, the Pinchots drove into Prineville, Oregon, for a church social. Mrs. Pinchot left me a pot of lamb stew and a glass of buttermilk. There were also, she pointed out in her friendliest manner, plenty of spiced apples and preserved cherries for my dessert; when they had gone I ate my supper on the dining room table in front of the familiar bowl of wax fruit. Then I did the dishes, put away the food and utensils, and settled down in the Pinchots' best over-stuffed chair with the telephone in my lap.

I dialed a familiar number in Mexico City. After four

rings someone answered.
"*Diga!*"
"Rufio?"
"Who?"
"Rufio, it's you. I can tell your voice."
"It's not Rufio, you *tonto*. It's Sergio." I had the wrong little brother. "Rufio's gone to dance class. He's nutty about the girls."
"Is mamá there?"
"Of course she is. Where else would she be? (A pause) Who are you?"
"Don't you recognize me? It's César-Agosto."
"César-Agosto?"
"Yes. And you're the *tonto* now. Call mamá."
There were screams at the other end of the line and then the breathless questions:
"Where are you, César-Agosto? Are you in China?"
"No."
"Japan?"
"No, I'm in the United States of America."
"Wow!" And more screams until mamá abruptly took over the receiver.
"Is that you, Agostino?"
"Yes, mamá."
"Are you in Montevideo?"
"No, mamá. I'm in Oregon."
"At your cousin Eduardo's? How is he? And Angelina, is she over her hip problems?"
"Mamá, Eduardo is in Nebraska. I'm phoning you from some place in Oregon."
"Where?"
"Oregon. In the United States."
"Well, why didn't you say so? All this time I thought you were at Eduardo's. *Callete!* (this to my brothers) That was Rufio. He just got back from wasting money

trying to *samba*. Where did you say you were? Rufio wants to know, too."

But I decided on a counterattack; it was dangerous getting into a rut with mamá.

"Is father there?"

"He's at the hotel. And, oh yes, Mr. Hyatt has made him his wine steward." My mother always personalized father's relations with that vast corporation—somehow it made his protracted absences from home more manageable to consider them interludes of important personal service.

"That's wonderful!"

"Of course, the appointment's only on trial. He'll probably fail to keep it. He has to memorize the names and something to say about ninety-six different wines and brandies. The man can't remember a grocery list. Agostino—"

"Yes, mamá?"

"Are you sure you're not at Eduardo's?"

"Eduardo lives in North Platte, Nebraska, mamá. I'm on a ranch in central Oregon. Working."

"Doing ranch work?"

"Yes." I didn't dare mention the dogs; it would have crushed her.

"You've given up tennis?"

"Just for now, mamá."

"I don't think that's wise, 'Tino. After all the time and money your father put into it. Anyone can be a *campesino* but to be a champion, even if you have to go to Uruguay to do it, even then—"

"Mamá," I broke in, "I haven't given it up. I'm just vacationing here."

"Then why didn't you say so?"

"I did."

"No, you didn't. Don't deceive your mother, 'Tino."

"Well, I thought I did."

"No, you said you were a *campesino* on someone's ranch."

"I was only joking."

Here we were, back at the old familiar game of reproach and defense. Nothing had really changed. When I was away from her long enough I always built up a sentimental image of my mother and filled it in with love and misapprehension, but the instant we were together the harsh truth intruded, and that truth was that we were condemned to forever antagonize and misunderstand each other. Then I knew why my father came home as little as possible, although his instincts had always been those of a family man.

"Mamá," I said desperately. "I phoned to find out where in San Diego the wedding party will be."

"Eduardo could get you a job selling cars. He manages the whole agency."

"Mamá," I repeated. "I need the address. It is important . . ."

"Wedding? Whose wedding?"

"Celestina Lourdes's. Your daughter's wedding."

"Oh, *that* wedding. It's September fourth."

"I know the date. But I need the *dirección*. I can't go unless I know where in San Diego it's going to be."

"You're phoning from Oregon? This must be costing you a fortune."

"Don't worry, mamá. It's on a credit card." She had never mastered the intricacies of credit cards; to her they were a form of divine intervention, like that of the Virgin Mary.

"Well, the wedding's not going to be in San Diego," she said triumphantly. "Marcantonio can't go back there—he's had a big argument with the Internal Revenue Service so they're getting married in Ensenada instead."

"The *dirección*?" I pleaded.
"Wait. I have it here somewhere." And after a long pause and much rustling of notebooks she gave it to me. "Your father is furious with Marcantonio," she added. "He refuses to go to the wedding." Marcantonio imported truckloads of Korean video equipment into Mexico; he had been living with my sister for three stormy years and I thought it a little late for my father to ostracize him.
"You'll have to represent the family, Agostino." Again the reproachful tone as if she knew in advance I would make a bad job of it.
"I know, mamá."
"When are you coming to Mexico City?"
"After the wedding, mamá."
"You can't do it before?"
"No, I can stop on my way to Montevideo. But not before."
"Your father will be very disappointed. He's always talking about . . ."
At that moment the line went dead so I never found out what he had in mind. I shook the receiver but nothing happened. I started to call the operator, then decided against it. I had found out what I wanted to know and if I got my mother on the line again it would surely turn out like one of those endless video loops where everything is always starting all over again from the beginning.
Instead, I dialled the Fridleys' house on Bainbridge Island. Right away I got Milo and his oatmeal accent.
Was Miss Fridley there?
Who?
Miss Sabrina Fridley.
I would have to speak a little louder, Milo informed me, apparently there was a bad connection. There was nothing wrong with our connection, I was sure—it was

only Milo's deafness, but I obliged him by shouting my beloved's name over the wires.

No, Miss Fridley was in Seattle for the evening.

No, he couldn't say when she would be available.

Yes, he would be happy to convey any message. In the morning.

Tell her—I yelled and then unaccountably fell silent.

Milo said that because of the static he didn't hear my message and would I mind repeating it?

I clicked the receiver and hung up. What good would it do?

It had been a day of missed connections.

I Get My Racquets Back

At breakfast I told the Pinchots I was leaving and, since they were going into Prineville for church services, I wondered if they would be kind enough to drop me off at the bus station. They agreed to do so, although Mrs. P. questioned the propriety of my travelling on the Sabbath. I told her that when I got to Klamath Falls I would attend evening services and that seemed to mollify her.

So I packed my few things, including the apples and the chunk of cheese Mrs. P. had pressed on me, made the bed and mopped the floor of the little room off the back entrance which had been my refuge for the past fortnight. I couldn't resist putting a note under the plumped-up pillow:

> If there are any extra charges, please take them out of the contingency fund.
> —Gus

I don't know whether it was an omen or not but the beagles in the first corral began a melancholy howling when they saw me get into the Pinchot's Studebaker. Pretty soon all the other hounds joined it and my departure from Pinchot Kennels was certainly more ceremonial than my arrival had been.

On the ten-mile drive to Prineville the Pinchots were largely silent but when we neared the bus station Mrs. P. asked where they could reach me if the need arose. I told her to write c/o the Y.M.C.A. in Klamath Falls. Mr. P. then expressed the hope that my sudden decision wasn't caused by our little disagreement of the day before and I assured him this was not the case and that homesickness for my family in Uruguay was what really motivated me. I then shook hands with them both and with the highest expressions of friendship and Christian regard we parted.

Two hours later I was in Bend, where I had been told there were a number of resorts which offered skiing in the winter and tennis in summer. It seemed at least possible that I might find some work at one of them. I had to do something as my money wouldn't stretch for both a summer in the United States and the flight back to Montevideo. And of course I also had it in mind to get back to Bainbridge Island when I could safely do so. With every day that passed the image of Sabrina became more wraith-like, a ghost from some past life which perhaps only Hindu transubstantiation could restore. But still I wanted to give it a try—we had been very close to something important, Sabrina and I, and I wasn't ready to close the books on it. I spent a day in Bend, making inquiries. Everyone was very friendly but it was still early June and in the northern mountains, they pointed out, that is too late for skiing but too early for the tennis crowd. In July, perhaps .... Of course July was too late for me. So I took the bus over the McKenzie Pass to Eugene, a gorgeous ride past still another volcano and down a famous trout stream through remarkable rain forests with an understory of dogwood and vine maple and the blossoms of trillium and adder's-tongue everywhere on the forest floor.

In Eugene I had a piece of luck—there was a local tournament in progress and among the seeds I saw the name of Nikki Fassmyer. I knew Nikki well; he had beaten me in Kobe and I had returned the compliment in Yokohama. So I strolled over to the side court where he was disposing of a local giant, 6-0, 6-1.

We gave each other the high five.

"Saint Nicholas!" He'd earned that nickname because he wasn't.

"Captain Straightarrow!" I'd gotten mine because I only drank Perrier on tour.

There is a splendid camaraderie that develops on the professional circuit and even if you lose all your matches you still share in it; you've been anointed, set apart from all the duffers and club players. Nikki and I were both authentic members—very junior members of course—of the fraternity of the famous or the about-to-become-famous, and as we shared in the honor we also shared the obligations. I was introduced to the ranking tennis-players, invited to share their board, and a bunk was found for me in the college dormitory where the visiting players were staying.

I was, of course, too late for the present tournament (where Nikki made it to the finals) but there were others coming up in Salem, Corvallis, and Medford where the managers would be delighted to have a one-time member of the Uruguayan Davis Cup squad. There would be expenses and some money too. "Of course, it's all under the table," Nikki said. "They know you don't have a green card. But it's cool, man. They *understand*." There was only one hitch: I had left my shoes and racquets, all my gear, in fact, with Steve at the Bainbridge club. But I saw that I had to bite the bullet sometime, so I took a chance and wired him.

Two days later I got back a note scrawled on the Bainbridge Tennis Club stationery:

> Dear Gus—
> Sorry dude the club manager says about the racquets no tickee no laundry. He claims you still owe 84 $ worth of saunas - sez pay up and we send your gear C.O.D. Its a cold cold world aint it?
> Your friend
STEVE

P.S.—hope you dont mind I gave Sabrina your address she sez she will write. Maybe she will *quien sabe?*

But she was as good as her word. The next day I got my racquets and shoes by Federal Express and inside the package there was a note:

Dear Agosto:

How completely unfair of them! The saunas were part of the treatment and should have been on *our* bill. I told Mr. Crofts I would resign from the club unless they gave me the racquets and that got *action.*

What a horrible scandal about Dr. Kains! I feel so sorry for his wife. All that time and the poor dear didn't know a thing! Can you believe it?

Do excuse me—in a dreadful rush as usual about something *utterly* unimportant.

It was signed with the familiar illegible squiggle.

I wrote back almost immediately. I didn't keep a copy so I don't remember much of my letter now but I am sure it was passionate and confused. I was in tears during much of the writing, swept up by a weird combination of love, anguish and gratitude for the safe return of my tennis racquets. Four days later I got this:

Dear Agosto:

How truly sweet of you to care so much! You're a perfect dear and I'm *immensely* flattered. Only you mustn't *write* such things.

That little sneak Cappy (he works for father you know) opens all the mail and I can tell from the way he leers that he thinks something torrid is going on. Ha, ha. So don't write, *please,* and you mustn't think of coming back to B.I. Mr. Harkins (he's father's counsel) says the District Attorney wants to question you and we'd better avoid that, he says. The trouble is that that *perfidious* Doctor K. put *all* our names down when he filed his flight plan in Winslow.

Vicki and I told them (*them* was a very nice detective who turned out to be a relative of Milo's) that *we all three* canceled out at the last minute but I still think he is curious about you—wanted to know if you were a Colombian and where and how we met you etcetera and so on. So, Agosto, do try not to be too conspicuous (you *inconspicuous*? I can hear you laughing) and don't write me any more letters. *Please*?

Now for the good news—Vicki has gotten her divorce and naturally her migraines are a lot better. And I am going to be in San Francisco sometime in early August and it's just possible we might see each other there, that is if you don't run off with someone with a better forehand between now and then.

Anyway, the phone is Area code 415, 426-0741 and they'll know when I'm coming in if I am at all because the whole trip is still iffy—depends a lot on father's mood and other *imponderables*. Cappy has given me Mann's *Magic Mountain* and I am reading it whatever chance I get. *Very* impressive! Naturally, I see a lot of myself in Hans Castorp (the hero I guess) particularly when he falls in love with the mysterious Russian lady after looking at her X-rays.

Cappy thinks I'm fascinated by people's diseases and after they get well or go away I'm off on another tangent. Part of my general decadence which comes from too much money for too many generations. That's his worm's-eye view of it. Theoretically he may be right but in weather like today's (all splashy sunlight and lilacs in bloom) I certainly don't *feel* decadent. And so on and so on and so forth . . . .

Sabrina

PHYLLIS

I grew to like Eugene very much. The town itself is attractive and it was a relief to be surrounded by so much lush greenery after the arid and dusty plains of Central Oregon. The western third of the state—the part between the ocean and the Cascade summit—is the damp part, with some localities along the coast getting as much as four meters of rain each year. But it was now mid-June, well into the dry season and we were favored by a long succession of warm, sunny days, ideal for tennis. My game rapidly improved and after ten days Nikki felt I was ready for some exhibition matches. We drove over to the coast in Nikki's VW camper and played matches, both singles and doubles, with the local champions. We won them all, but discovered an especially good match-up in our doubles games—Nikki took the net with great authority while I have always been a strong back-court player, able to run hard and return almost anything. At night we camped out among the sand dunes and went clam-digging on a long beach at Yachats. Driving back to Eugene through the fir forests of the coast range Nikki commented on how much it reminded him of the Black Forest in Germany, "only without the castles." Nikki's father was a pilot with Lufthansa and although Nikki himself is thoroughly American he spoke German and had travelled a lot in Europe. Nikki's mother, Phyllis, was an artist who lived near Eugene. She was married now to a tax attorney named Albert Holiwell. Nikki lived in town and didn't see her all that frequently; he never referred to her as *mamá* or *mother*, just as "Phyllis." He stood in a good deal of awe of his stepfather. "Wait till you meet him," he told me. "The man does everything. He's an absolute genius. Repulsive, but a genius."

But first I was to be exposed to Phyllis. I had seen her in the stands and around the court when Nikki was playing—a small, trim, dark-eyed woman who looked much younger than her age. She was given to dressing in raw silk pantsuits with broad-brimmed straw hats and a wild variety of chiffon scarves in colors with outrageous names like puce, gamboge, mauve and azure. Then one day I got a note from her asking if I would meet her at Zambini's, a rather *chic* restaurant near the University, for lunch. "My guest, of course," she scrawled at the bottom, sensitive as she must have been to the state of my purse.

"I wanted to t-t-talk to you about Nikki," she said after she had ordered the Dover sole and a bottle of Chardonnay. "I'm worried about him."

But before I report what she said and didn't say about her son I want to describe her in more detail. We were to become (and remain) very dear friends and what I have to say is of course not the result of any one meeting. And should she ever chance to read this (which isn't likely) I hope she won't be offended.

Phyllis was not greatly verbal; in fact, she was inclined to stammer and she hated all abstract words and generalizations. But the words she did use she handled like a master actor, coloring each with the emotion the moment demanded. She used the word *yes*, for example, a great deal, often as many as five or six of them in a row, yet her range of inflection and shading was so great she could convey dozens of quite different meanings by that one syllable. Similarly with *no*, although in the course of events it occurred less frequently for Phyllis was generally a *positive* person.

She lived in a world where each happening, no matter how workaday its surface, had emotional significance. She was profoundly *simpático* and her empathy extended to all things, animal, vegetable or mineral. Normally so endearing, this trait could be profoundly disturbing as well when, for instance, you realized that Phyllis genuinely felt the anguish of the flat stone you had just skipped across the Willamette and shivered too with the water's torn skin. With Phyllis one was constantly reminded of the pain lurking behind every joy; even in her gayest moments she was always somehow on the edge of tears. This made every conversation with her something of a trial; Phyllis had no "small talk"—with her even the most casual and quotidian remark was linked to the Great Chain of Being and hence was capable of inflicting either joy or suffering, often both together.

Also, Phyllis was constantly touching you as she talked, not, I think, with any of the obvious intentions behind such gestures, but to reassure herself that you were really there, as if only by physical sensation could she overcome her *absences*, her inner conviction that all life was at best an insubstantial veil surrounding a core of nothingness. So when she took your hand as you talked to her you wanted to return the warm pressure because it would be cruelty not to.

Was this response of mine sexual? Of course. But then *everything* was sexual with Phyllis. And *not* sexual. The two were hopelessly entangled. Which was a part of her fascination.

Now she talked of Nikki's breakup with his girl friend, something that had happened a few days before I arrived in Eugene. She seemed to hold herself responsible for it.

"I know Enzel felt th-threatened by me," she said.

"She never said anything, no, no, that wasn't her way. But it was there, yes, hanging between us. I could sense it." Enzel was the only name I ever heard for Nikki's girl—she was a musician and apparently felt a single name more effective in the clubs. Anyway, she had walked out on Nikki without notice; he didn't know where she was and professed not to care. I had never heard from him that Phyllis had anything to do with the rupture.

"Perhaps Nikki has talked to you about it?"

"Hardly at all," I said quite truthfully.

"I don't want you to vi-violate any confidences," she said in her husky, slightly breathless voice, a voice which seemed always poised on the edge of some startling revelation if only she could remember *precisely* what it was.

"We're perfectly safe," I said with a laugh. "Nikki so far hasn't confided in me."

"Oh . . . in that case . . . ."

What was she asking me to do? To spy on her son and report back to her? I wasn't at all sure.

"Enzel was so perfect for him. I couldn't f-face myself if I thought . . . . I've been such a *wr-wretched* mother to Nikki . . . ."

Naturally, I tried to reassure her.

"No, no, no, it's true, it's true," she whispered and took my hand across the table. He has every reason to d-d-despise me. I was unfair to Enzel, I know it. But Agosto," she pleaded, "don't you despise me. I couldn't bear that."

I told her she could count on me through thick and thin.

She took out a filmy azure handkerchief and brushed away a tear. "Yes! Yes!" she cried, "We'll be friends, won't we?" and then with a sweeping gesture upset my wine glass.

As we stanched up the resultant mess it suddenly

occurred to me that this dramatic luncheon was staged entirely for my benefit and had nothing at all to do with the wayward Nikki. A disloyal thought, yes, but one that refused to go away.

Two days later she summoned Nikki and me to her house on the banks of the Willamette River. Today she was dressed in a black velveteen pantsuit with a cerise scarf about her throat; with this costume she was barefoot and I was surprised to see an amethyst ring on one toe of her slender foot. She showed me through the house which was modern, large, and had a lot of glass. The walls were crowded with her paintings and constructions which Nikki had warned me sold in New York and Los Angeles for astronomically high prices. The house and the art work obviously bored Nikki; he made a point of sitting on one of Phyllis's tubular chrome chairs reading a copy of *Sports Illustrated* which I suspected he had brought along just to flaunt in his mother's face.

The sculptures were a shock, particularly coming from such an apparently frail and tentative person as Phyllis chose to appear. For the most part they were huge squares of rough-cast aluminum framed in chrome or blonde wood. Phyllis explained the process: molten aluminum was poured into moulds constructed of burlaps and gauzes stiffened with wire and plaster. Pieces of charred cloth along with fragments of bronze were embedded in the finished *bas-reliefs*. Sections of the gray oxidized aluminum were pitted in a sort of moonscape, others had been ground smooth and then scribed with mysterious hieroglyphs. I glimpsed a few titles—*Scoriac #12, Space Landing* and *Desert Scape* were typical. In some of them weird metal fixtures, either mushrooms or typewriter keys, I couldn't decide which, had been screwed into the surface. It was international high-style art at its most chilling. And powerful. I couldn't believe that

Phyllis could be the artist.

She sensed my incredulity and hastened to explain. "Of course I don't p-p-personally do the foundry work. I have a couple of dear old Italians who pour the metal." Still, the construction of the elaborate moulds represented more physical labor than I would have thought her capable of.

"When the fire is in you," she said, "nothing seems too hard. Don't you feel that too, Agosto?"

She had touched something in me with that question. "Yes," I said. "Yes."

In a farther room we came upon some hand-woven wall hangings which looked very South American. I remarked on the contrast between their strong use of reds and yellows as compared to the monochromes of the raw aluminum pieces.

"Oh, but they are Albert's, not mine."

"Albert?"

"My husband."

"Your husband weaves?" This was very far from the image I had formed of Albert Holiwell, tax lawyer.

"Albert does everything," she said proudly. "But weaving is his p-p-passion. It relaxes him."

I said that to my eyes his work seemed highly professional.

She pressed my hand. "Tell him that. Yes, please do. People don't realize what a fine artist Albert is." I could see a tear forming again in the corner of her eye. "It's not easy for him, no, it's not easy being married to a painter. To me, I mean. Being married to me is not always easy, Agosto."

I said that a challenging life was what made you grow, or words to that effect.

"Yes, yes—yes! You are so right, Agosto." And with a quick, impulsive movement, she kissed me on the cheek and then, barefoot, pirouetted away across the carpet.

We rejoined Nikki who yawned ostentatiously over his magazine.

When it came time to leave she stood in the doorway and took both my hands in hers.

"Please come again," she said in her husky voice. "Nikki, you must bring your friend back. You mustn't desert us. There are so few people with whom one can talk, yes, really talk. And Albert will be furious that he missed you. Yes, furious."

ALBERT

"There's someone waiting for you outside."
"Who is it?"
"How should I know?"
"Well, what does he look like?"
"Official."
I shivered. Perhaps from the cold shower I had just taken. Perhaps not. I was getting dressed after some intensive practice. The messenger was one of my housemates in the old shingled dormitory where I was temporarily living.
"How can you tell?"
"Intuition. He's fat. Placid. Has a calculator. Go see for yourself."
I wasn't in any hurry; right away I thought of the Seattle district attorney and his minions.
"Is there a back exit?" I asked, only half joking.
"Maybe it's the building inspector, that's what he looks like. It's certainly time they condemned this place. It's a zoo."
I slipped on my windbreaker and went outside, whistling. Sure enough, there was a stout, gray-haired man waiting for me on the porch. He had tufted eyebrows and a round, pink, scrubbed face like a baby's. He wore a pistachio-green *guayabera* shirt and khaki trousers. The day was hot and he was sweating heavily.
"You're Agosto?" he asked.
I admitted that much.
He mumbled his own name but at that moment the Fairmont bus rumbled past, blotting it out. My mind was awhirl with plausible answers to the questions I felt sure were just over the horizon poised to fall on

me like a posse of vengeful cavalrymen.

"My wife says you are Uruguayan."

"What?"

"She says you are from Uruguay. In South America."

What on earth had this man's wife to do with me? I stared stupidly at the row of clip-pens and the electronic calculator in the top pockets of his *guayabera*.

"My wife, Phyllis."

"Phyllis is your wife?" I was astounded. He offered me his hand.

"I'm Albert. Albert Holiwell."

Astounded, yes, but also extremely relieved.

We walked across campus to the Student Union where he bought us iced tea which we drank on the terrace outside under a sun-umbrella. I told him I had taken him for an immigration officer and he roared with laughter. He laughed a great deal, I was to find out, perhaps because fat men are supposed to be jolly or perhaps because laughter was his way of coping with a complex and not altogether satisfying life.

"You seemed so interested in my nationality."

"I am," he said. "But I have more amusing reasons for my curiosity. How did it come about?"

"What?"

"Your Uruguayishness, if I may coin a horrible word."

"I emigrated. From Mexico." I explained the circumstances. When I was twelve years old and already showed promise at tennis, my coach, Don Pablo Uriarte, convinced my father that it would jeopardize my career to remain in Mexico. The air was unbreathable and the strain of jetting in and out of a city 2500 meters above sea level would endanger my heart, or so he said. My father set great store by Uncle Pablo's advice and when he offered to take me to Montevideo with him the proposal seemed too good to decline. So I went to school in Uruguay and when I turned out to be good enough to make their Davis Cup squad the tennis federation said I'd have to become an Uruguayan. That was it. I was naturalized. One passport is as good as another.

"Remarkable," Mr. Holiwell said. "A really bizarre coincidence." He offered no further explanation but fell silent and began staring at the campus lawns around us. After a while I started to speak but he halted me with an upraised hand on which I was startled to notice four hammered silver rings, one for each finger.

"Listen!" he commanded. There was a low hiss like that of a far-off wind. "Wait! A moment now." His ringed hand paused in the air and then, like a conductor summoning the entrance of a string section, he brought it swiftly down. At that precise beat all the lawn sprinklers began whirling their watery sprays.

"Magical, isn't it?"

"You heard that coming?" I was truly astounded.

"Every happening," he said magisterially, "casts its aura both before and after its arrival. Your shadow walks ahead of you in the morning, underfoot at noon, and follows behind in the evening. In this case," he admitted, "it was also the air pressure building up in the pipes. One can learn to detect and predict it."

"You are a *brujo*," I said with admiration.

"A warlock," Mr. Holiwell responded. "And not very high in the profession." He heaved his sweating bulk out of the chair, as if to signal that our interview was over. On his feet he had an afterthought: "Oh yes—my wife and I have an empty garden cottage. If you would care to be our guest during your stay in Eugene, we would be honored."

I realized then that he must have been sent by Phyllis on an errand he could not have found completely congenial. But for me it was opportune—I had just been given notice at the dormitory. So I accepted with one of my best Spanish bows.

"I hope it doesn't discommode you, sir."

"Not at all. I look forward to our conversations. And later on," he added with a mischievous smile, "we will talk, you and I, about what it means to be Uruguayan."

So I moved out to the banks of the Willamette. Phyllis bought me some new clothes and Albert loaned me a little Fiat when I needed to run into town. They were wonderful to me; I had suddenly acquired a new family and it made me very happy.

Only Nikki didn't approve of the arrangement.

"Watch out for Phyllis," he warned me. "She's a man-eater."

I thought this an impolite way to talk about one's own mother but I wasn't going to spoil my general mood of euphoria by arguing.

"I'll take care," I said. "I'm not going to be a sandwich."

Nikki and I had signed up for the Oregon state championships in Salem. We thought we had a chance for the prize money—particularly Nikki in the singles. He was playing at the top of his game that summer; he put it down to his girl's leaving.

"Enzel was a strain," he said. "She was too much of too much."

Nikki professed to like the quiet life. His mother's intensity annoyed him and Enzel had been just as disturbing in another way. I asked him about his father, the Lufthansa pilot.

"Oh, for a German he's laid back," Nikki said. "Of course that's not saying too much. I think what I really need is a hammock, a tequila sunrise and Miss America fanning my toes with a banana leaf."

"Preferably speechless."

"You're fucking well right. Speechless, that's the only way."

Nikki was coarse but despite the facade I knew he had been badly hurt by Enzel's rejection. In Japan he had talked a lot about her, her intelligence and beauty, her resourcefulness, her skill on the harmonica, recorder and even the Irish penny-whistle. Now of course he had nothing good to say of her, but that was Nikki's way—he was just as high-strung and given to extremes as his mother but while she exploited it, he lived by denying it.

Somewhere between them stood Albert, a strange and often contradictory alloy of impulse and shrewdness.

When Albert left law school he had gone to work as an agent at the Internal Revenue Service. "Walpurgis Night," he told me. "The Day of the Dead stretched out over seven years. Every day I was there I learned a new variation on suffocation." Then one December afternoon in Philadelphia he had come across three Jamaican children building a snowman out of the first snowfall they had ever seen. The play-demon, which had been stifled for so long that he had grown to think it dead burst out—he threw down his overcoat and briefcase and stuck his hat on the snowman. Apparently he had not completely lost his inherited magical powers; the children accepted him and all afternoon they played together in the snow. "I frolicked," Albert said. "That's the only word for it." His strange conduct was observed and reported to his department. He was ordered to take psychological tests and refused to appear. As a result he was declared mentally unfit for the IRS. "It was a perfect mutual diagnosis," he told me. "They thought I had gone mad, and I knew they had always been crazy. Actually, I had been transformed and I wasn't going back to that house of evil under any circumstances." So, in the ongoing war between taxpayer and tax collector, he had shifted his allegiance to the other side; now he counselled the rich on strategies to defeat his old department's rapacity.

Albert wasn't at the house very much; he worked hard at his business and he also had a cabin in the mountains where he kept his loom and often spent days in silent shuttling, but when he was around he was very kind to me. Of course he knew that I was his wife's favorite but even that didn't so much as stir a ripple in his serenity. We went for tramps along the flood embankments and he showed me the powers of his white magic over wild creatures, how he could walk up to the mallards and with a low chirring noise calm them so that they allowed him to ruffle their feathers; how by whistling he could coax the gophers and ground squirrels from their burrows in the levee. White magic could not be used, he explained, to trap or kill any creature.

So it surprised me when he suggested we visit his country club, since a *club campestre* in Latin-America is a place where huntsmen gather to shoot doves or pheasant or wild pigs. He told me that in the United States "country clubs" are exclusively devoted to the well-known northern game of *golf*.

"Do you play it?" I asked.

"Good God, no!" He exploded with mirth. "It's utter foolishness." But since all of his clients either played or pretended to it was essential that he keep up a membership. It was as much a part of the front he put up as the burgundy-colored Cadillac in which we drove to the club or the ridiculous Hawaiian sports shirt he chose for the occasion.

"It's all protective coloration, my camouflage. And remember, Agosto, no talk of magic, no *brujos* today. They wouldn't be appreciated."

At the club everyone knew him as "Al"; there was much indiscriminate jesting and back-slapping, at which he seemed to be expert. We sat on the terrace overlooking the 18th hole and again drank only iced tea (he was on a strict non-alcoholic diet; I think he suffered from diabetes). Albert made wicked *sotto voce* comments on the various silly personages descending from their electrified golf carts and I shared his merriment.

After a time we were joined by a ruddy, sweating gentleman whom I assumed was one of his clients. He was introduced to me as "Bill" and gave me one of his business cards. It read

> William P. ("Bill") Wetherall
> President, Bay States Shrimp Farms Inc.

There was no address, only a telephone number.

Mr. Wetherall ordered a Scotch-and-branchwater and removed his golf cap. His skin from mid-forehead up was a pale pink, while from that point down it was brick red; it looked as if the top of his skull had been sawed off and replaced by another.

"Agosto is the Uruguayan friend I told you about," Albert said.

Mr. Wetherall grinned and gave me a crushing handshake. "Hi, young feller, what's your handicap?"

"Handicap?"

"Agosto doesn't play golf," Albert explained.

"Not play golf?" It seemed unthinkable.

I nodded dumbly.

"He's from South America."

"Oh," said Mr. Wetherall, everything clear now, "the Underdeveloped Countries." Then he cheered up. "I'll have to teach him, won't I, Al?"

We all agreed that this was a fine idea. I waved expansively toward the golf course and said, "I admire all these beautiful green lawns. I should be most happy to stroll on them."

Mr. Wetherall looked at me dubiously. "They won't let you walk, young feller, you have to rent a cart. Pedestrians slow down the game too much."

"The players here have to hurry up to relax," Albert said, deadpan, and winked at me.

But I was suddenly too depressed to wink back.

I Become a Tycoon

"You must do as Albert says," Phyllis told me. "Albert is wiser than any of us."

"Thank you, my dear," Albert said brushing *croissant* crumbs from his *Wall Street Journal*.

"But it's true! Albert sees farther than you and I, Agosto. Albert has—"

"Prescience," her husband supplied.

"Exactly. And if Albert says you must play golf with that horrible Mr. Wetherall, then you must do it. And don't be sulky about it, dear."

This morning Phyllis was dressed, charmingly, in French workman's blue coveralls and wore a magenta scarf in her hair. Around her neck a pair of industrial goggles, ugly in themselves, managed to look *chic*. Phyllis was on her way to the foundry for a day of casting.

"I put some clubs in the back of the Fiat," Albert said. "The wooden ones are for your first shots, the weird square one is the putter and you are to use it only on the greens."

Phyllis was at the door. "Replace your divots!" she called gaily. "Whatever *they* are." And was gone.

"I wasn't sulking," I explained to my host. "Actually, I look forward to the challenge."

"You'll do well. Just listen politely to whatever nonsense he tells you and keep your eye on the ball. Play well if you can but not too well. And if you have to choose between appearing bright or stupid opt for stupidity every time."

I said I would follow his advice but that I had a

question or two of my own.

He anticipated me: "Naturally you want to know *why*. What the old *brujo* was up to, eh?"

I nodded.

"We are all about to make some money, Agosto," he said solemnly. "Quite a lot of money. But first you must win Mr. Wetherall's approval. Mr. Wetherall never does business with strangers."

"And he and I are going to do business?"

"I think so, Agosto, I think so." And here he adjusted his horn-rimmed glasses and returned to his paper, only to re-emerge when I had finished my coffee and was almost at the door. "By the way, Agosto, don't ask him any questions about the shrimp farms. It's a sensitive topic."

*

We met again, for dinner, at a Szechuan restaurant in downtown Eugene.

"I did the course in ninety-six blows," I reported.

"Not bad, not bad," Albert mumbled, deep in the intricacies of the menu.

"I think it's fabulous!" Phyllis turned admiring brown eyes on me. "Think of that, Albert, and only his first time ever."

"Mmmhmmm."

"I also upset the electric golf cart in a sand trap. Mr. Wetherall was very nice about it. We righted it and pushed it out. There was only a little bend in the axle."

The waiter approached and Albert ordered expertly for all of us, starting with *mushu* pork and rice-flour crepes.

"Don't forget, darling, I want some *sake*," Phyllis said, touching him affectionately on the forearm. Tonight she was dressed in a pure white *sari* with gold trim.

She wore a number of gold bangles and a choker wrought in the form of a snake. She looked quite the aging Cleopatra.

"Unfortunately this place is Chinese not Japanese. No *sake*, I'm afraid. There's a Hungarian green wine. Will that do?"

"He spoke very highly of you."

"Who?"

"Mr. Wetherall."

"It will have to," said Phyllis, coming up from the menu. "There's nothing else worth drinking. Only Hong Kong beer and you know how I feel about *that*."

"He said," I put in, "that you are a genuine financial wizard."

"Little does he know!" Phyllis said gaily; then swiftly changed her mood. "Look, darlings, I was burned today." She pulled the bangles up her arm and displayed two tiny circular burns on her wrist. "Aluminum sparks. They're horribly hot. I took the leather glove off, just for a second, yes, that's all, and there was this spatter. It hurt a lot. At the time." She dabbed at the tears the memory of pain had brought.

"Looks like a vampire bite to me," Albert said with mock gloom.

"Your *mushu* pork," the waiter announced. "With plum sauce for the pancakes."

"Which brings me," said Albert, "to an announcement." He waited for us to quiet down. "Agosto today is about to become—"

"Wait! Let me guess! Ch-chiropodist? A p-p-pastry chef? A professional golfer?"

"No, my dear. A business tycoon."

"A what?"

"A tycoon. A captain of industry. A robber of the poor. I've been on the phone with Bill Wetherall. He has just approved Agosto's appointment as a board member of Plains of Plenty, Inc." He poured the Hungarian wine in all our glasses. "It is a time of rejoicing. A time for festivity."

"Oh, Agosto," Phyllis cried. "I'm so happy for you." She leaned over the table and kissed me. "We're all going to be rich together!"

"He thinks you are thoroughly charming. I think it was upsetting the golf cart that did it." Albert attacked his crepe with gusto; apparently he had forgotten all about his diet for the green wine began to disappear with alarming speed.

"How wonderful for you, dear Agosto." Phyllis hovered on the edge of tears.

I protested that I knew nothing at all about business.

"Of course you don't," said Albert. "Wetherall saw that at a glance—it's one of your great assets. He only wants to borrow your name. You are to be, how is it called in Spanish?"

"A *prestanombre*?"

"Exactly. Or more vulgarly in English: a *stand-in*."

"I stand in? For what?"

"For glory. For national sovereignty. You, Agosto, are to be our token Uruguayan. There are no duties. There is no risk. There are only fees. Regular board fees. Let us start with this."

He handed me a check on the account of Plains of Plenty, Inc., made out to me in the amount of $3,000.00. It was signed by William P. Wetherall as secretary-treasurer.

"I will of course take you to the bank tomorrow so that you can convert this into cash."

Naturally, I was dumbfounded. "But what is Plains of Plenty?"

"I will give you as many of the grim details as you

want tomorrow. For now let me say only that as fellow board members, Agosto, you and I and Mr. Wetherall are honorably engaged in the cattle business." He paused, wiped his mouth with a napkin, then added significantly, "In Uruguay."

"Listen to him, Agosto," Phyllis said tearfully. "Albert is going to make your fortune."

Albert was protective. "Enough sobbing, dear. This is a joyous occasion. Let us proceed to attack the chicken *kung-pao!*"

The waiter stood by in amazement as he helped himself to more than half the steaming platter.

*

At the bank in the morning I presented the check, Albert vouched for my endorsement, and the cashier handed over thirty crisp one hundred dollar bills without so much as a raised eyebrow. We then went to Albert's office where I signed a number of papers and Albert explained the scheme to me. As well as I can remember, these are the essential details:

Plains of Plenty was a Delaware corporation engaged in shipping Black Angus breeding stock and premium Danish milch cows to various ranch brokers around the world, but primarily in South America. The company then packaged and sold to investors 'limited partnerships' in these cattle. Because of the short life expectancy of beef cattle, American investors were able to claim extremely high first-year depreciations on their partnerships, often amounting to two or three hundred percent of their cash outlay. The partnerships, then, were designed as tax shelters for the wealthy and were racking up millions in sales.

During the previous year Plains of Plenty had acquired some 5,000 acres of range land in the Paysandu District of Uruguay along the Argentine border and had set up a sister corporation as the legal owner of these properties. This was called Llanas Llenas, S.A., with offices in Montevideo. Under Uruguayan law a majority of the directors had to be citizens. There were two in place: one I shall call only Señor Z, since he was and is a very highly placed politician in Uruguay and even I, who am a total ignoramus in politics, had heard of him; the other was Sr. Gavino Petronelli, chairman of the Fondo Agropecuario of Montevideo and one of the country's most aggressive bankers. His task was to manage the actual settling of cattle on the Paysandu land and also to promote development loans from the government banks. These two directors would have been happy to supply the necessary fifth director from among their cronies but Albert clearly saw the danger there and wasn't about to allow it to happen. A third Uruguayan director who would "listen to reason" was essential before the project could safely continue.

"At this precise moment you appeared," Albert said. "It was a miracle. If I hadn't known better, I would have said that I had conjured you out of thin air." Then he left me with two serious warnings: first and most obviously, if the board of Llanas Llenas were ever to divide I was to vote promptly and without question with Albert; secondly, I was to say nothing about my new position, at least until I was back in Uruguay where it would soon be a matter of public knowledge. "But not a word while you're in the United States, Agosto. We don't want the Immigration Service mixed in this one."

At that moment my trust in and admiration for Albert Holiwell was at its zenith. I signed every document he presented and gave him my word without reservations. He was a magician, *un gran brujo*, and I was his grateful disciple.

CHAMPION AT LAST

Good luck runs in cycles. Only ten days after I became a board member of Llanas Llenas, S.A., in the midst of a record-breaking heat wave in the capital city of Salem, Nikki and I became the doubles champions of the State of Oregon. Our reward was a gold-plated trophy which I let Nikki keep, a lot of publicity ("Eugene Man Teams with Paraguayan for Doubles Crown," one headline read) and one thousand dollars which we split. As soon as the tournament was over I headed north.

"Tell Phyllis I'll be back in a week," I instructed Nikki. It was no more than polite to keep her posted—after all, I was driving the Holiwell's Fiat.

"Where are you going?"

"I left some unfinished business in Seattle," I said in my best imitation of a John Wayne drawl.

"Good luck."

"Thanks, pardner."

I was now a comparatively rich man, drove a car, had a job (of a nebulous sort, it's true) and was an authentic American sports champion with the clippings to prove it. In my dream life this made my return to Bainbridge Island so triumphant that even the Fridleys, walled about by their snobbishness, could not fail to be impressed. The King County district attorney, too, would see his dreadful mistake and offer abject apologies. This at least was my fantasy scenario. It was not, unfortunately, to survive past Portland.

Ever since passing Oregon City I had sensed I was being followed by two men in a charcoal Buick. I sped up, so did they; I lagged, they followed suit. So I took the Tualatin off-ramp and parked in a service station where there were plenty of witnesses and waited to see what they had in mind. They drove alongside, got out and walked over to me. They had plain-clothes police written all over them.

"Mr. Villasenor?"

"Yes."

"Mr. Cesar Villasenor?" He pronounced my first name "Seize-her."

I winced but said yes.

"Your driver's license and passport, please."

"And who are you?" I countered.

"Immigration and Naturalization," the lead officer said, flashing a badge clipped to his wallet. It was just like the movies, down to the bow-ties and snap-brim hats. I often think American police agents study their roles from television. Anyway, my papers were in order so I handed over my international driver's license and passport. They passed them one to the other in silent scrutiny but made no move to give them back.

"Get back in your car, sir," the first one finally said, "and follow us downtown."

The second one offered the classic line: "And don't try any funny business, Buster."

I followed them into the center of Portland and we entered the basement garage of an eleven-story steel-and-concrete building. We rode the elevator in silence to the eighth floor where I was relieved of my billfold, car-keys and pocket knife by a bored lady officer. We then took the elevator back to the third floor where I was given a receipt for them, then up to the fifth floor where I was ushered into a very comfortable interview room and offered a cigarette.

"Sorry, I don't smoke."

"Very wise of you," the senior officer said. He introduced himself as Frank Gosby; his associate, he said, was Roger Mullowney. They were almost interchangeable except that Mr. Gosby did all the talking and had a stubbly pepper-and-salt moustache.

"We don't want you to jump to any conclusions, Seizeher," Mr. Gosby said in a friendly, fatherly tone. "You're not under arrest, just temporary detention."

"Excuse me, sir, but I don't see the difference."

"Under detention," Mr. Gosby explained, "the subject is invited in to answer a few questions. Under arrest the subject's departure may be prevented by the appropriate use of physical force."

"Then I am free to walk out of here whenever I want?"

"Of course. Although as a friend, I wouldn't advise it."

"Why not?"

"The commissioner might then—notice, I only say *might*—consider your arrest and deportation warranted."

"In which case physical force might be used to restrain me?"

"Conceivably," said Mr. Gosby softly, "it might."

"Then let's get on with it," I said amiably.

Mr. Gosby rubbed his hands together with satisfaction. "Excellent. Make a note of that, Roger."

"Check," said Mr. Mullowney, scribbling. "Subject agrees to voluntary interrogation."

"First," Mr. Gosby said, "let me ask you if you would care to have an interpreter."

"What for?"

"I thought perhaps you might be more at home in Spanish."

"Is there something wrong with my English?" His question really irritated me as I am very proud of my fluent English.

"Not at all," he hastened to assure me. "You speak excellent English. In fact, we were commenting in the hall on how well you spoke English, weren't we, Roger?"

"That we were," said Mr. Mullowney. "Remarkable grasp of English."

"Then we will proceed," Mr. Gosby said, that matter settled all around. He then asked me a number of the usual questions—where I had been, when I had entered the country, how I had enjoyed my stay—before he got down to business.

"We don't in any way want or desire to interfere with your visit to our great country, Seize-her. Tourists of your type and, well, educational background are always more than welcome. And we're very glad to have sportsmen of your quality take part in our tournaments. However, as you well know, non-resident aliens are expressly forbidden to receive remuneration for any and all forms of gainful activity during their sojourn in the States. Our information is that you may have—whether wittingly or unwittingly, that's up to the Commissioner to determine—violated these statutes by the acceptance of fees, prizes and/or remuneration for your services as a sportsman."

"Can you be more specific, sir?"

"I'm afraid not, Seize-her. Specific charges with supporting documents and testimony will be presented if and when there is a deportation hearing and not before. That's the law and it's for your protection."

"In that case, sir," I said coolly, "I don't think I ought to respond to your questions without the presence of my attorney."

"I'm sorry you look at it that way, Seize-her," Mr. Gosby said, a genuine sense of loss creasing his face. "I had looked forward to a friendly chat."

"It will have to wait, sir," I said and passed him one of Albert's cards which he had given me for just such an emergency. Mr. Gosby read it and passed it on to Mr. Mullowney for his inspection as well.

"Mr. Albert J. Holiwell is your legal counsel?"

"He is."

"An eminent member of the bar," Mr. Gosby allowed.

"You know him?"

"Yes, we've had differences of opinion with Counsellor Holiwell on several occasions." He sighed. "I think we should recess now, Roger. We have a number of things to take up with the Commissioner." He turned back to me. "Put your feet up on the sofa if you like and have a snooze. You'll find V-8 juice in the fridge. And there's *salsa* music on the tape machine—many of your people enjoy it. We'll be back soon."

"Thank you, sir," I said. "But there *is* one other courtesy I would appreciate."

"Yes?"

"Could I phone the sports editor of the Portland *Oregonian*? I'm sure he would like to know how I'm doing."

If that shot got to him he was too cool to show it. "I doubt if that will be necessary, Mr. Villasenor," he said pleasantly. And left.

They were back in forty minutes, all beaming smiles and congratulations as if I had just won the lottery.

"You're on your way, young man," Mr. Gosby said, clapping me affectionately on the shoulder. "Roger, go with him and see that he gets his possessions back."

"I am free?"

"You've always been free since you never were in *de jure* custody. However, the Commissioner agreed with us that this visit should be considered a warning only. We have called your attention to the applicable statutes and now it's up to you. Be careful. Next time around the Commissioner may not be so lenient." He shook my hand heartily. "Good luck, Mr. Villasenor. Are you going to visit Disneyland?"

"I hadn't thought of it, sir."

"Don't miss it. Disneyland and the Grand Canyon—they're irreplaceable."

Mr. Mullowney accompanied me to the third floor to exchange my receipt for a release order, then up to the eighth to get my papers, money and car-keys. In the elevator Mr. Mullowney finally broke his prolonged silence.

"I told the chief all along you weren't the type," he confided.

"The type?"

"You know," he said significantly, "the *type*."

"I'm sorry, but I don't know."

"The type we're on the lookout for. You don't fit it. You've got the wrong profile."

I didn't know whether this was a compliment or not, so I was silent. In the garage Mr. Gosby reappeared for final farewells and instructions on regaining the freeway.

"By the way," he said as I was about to start up the Fiat, "you're going to have to find yourself a new attorney."

I asked him what he meant.

"I'm afraid your Mr. Holiwell is deceased."

"Dead?" I was stunned. Albert the magician dead in an instant?

"Yes," said Mr. Gosby. "He has passed away. It's in the morning papers. A tragic accident. Involving a tree, I think."

I drove out of the garage and stopped on the first corner for a paper. Gosby was right. There it was—Prominent Attorney Victim of Freak Accident." An eighty foot Douglas fir had fallen on his mountain cabin and killed him instantly. The account then grew eloquent: "Mr. Holiwell, whose avocation was weaving for which he had won many awards, was seated at his loom when Death knocked."

I drove through Portland in a daze. All thought of the Fridleys had vanished. When I came to the freeway I took the southern direction and drove as fast as I could. Toward Eugene.

Some Farewells

The funeral was simple but moving. The Theosophy Hall had been rented for the occasion and the elegy was delivered by a Dr. Lachlan of the Humanist Society who pointed up the rare blend of idealism, artistic talent, and moral probity which had been lost by the tragic death of Mr. Holiwell. I thought he spoke in very good taste and without the exaggeration so common at funerals. There was organ music, and Nikki and I supported Phyllis who wept of course ("she couldn't possibly miss the opportunity," Nikki whispered cynically afterwards) but she didn't overdo it. The pallbearers, among them Mr. Wetherall, were from the country club and the financial community; there were also a great many Holiwell cousins and aunts among the mourners. The body was incinerated and nobody got to watch that except the widow and she declined. I think I should have accepted had I been in her place; they say the process is very interesting and the last memory of your husband or wife as a blue-and-red flame must be worth treasuring. But then we Latinos are closer to our dead than the North Americans—early death is certainly much more familiar to us.

After the ceremony Bill Wetherall asked me into the Elks Club bar for a Scotch whiskey, which I drank out of courtesy to the dead.

"A great man gone to his reward," he observed solemnly. "We won't see his like soon. Not in our lifetime."

I agreed that our loss was irreparable.

He offered me another whiskey which I politely declined.

"I know Al thought the world of you, young feller." A fly buzzed around his balding head where the sweatband of his fedora had left its mark and at last settled on the rim of his whiskey glass. He seemed at a loss for words.

"I guess he was a sort of uncle to you," he said finally. "Took you into his home. Advanced your career."

"He was very kind to me."

"Young feller, I want you to think of me the same way. If you're ever in trouble or need a helping hand—"

"You've already been too generous, sir."

"—there's more where that came from," he said and finished his second whiskey.

I told him I appreciated his thoughtfulness and asked him what I ought to do about my directorships in Plains of Plenty and its South American subsidiary.

"Just sit tight," he said emphatically. "Sit tight. Uruguay is going to have to go on the back burner now that Al is gone but I'll let you know when you're needed. Just sit tight."

He gave me another business card—*Imperial Consolidated Inc.*, with an address on Sutter Street in San Francisco. "An import firm I've got a piece of," he explained. "Mexican leather goods. They can always reach me if you need help. Look me up any time." He signed his tab, we shook hands and parted as the best of friends.

I went round to Nikki's apartment to pick up a racquet I had loaned him while his were being restrung. I was taking the bus to San Francisco the next morning. Eugene was all over for me. Nikki seemed depressed.

"Guess who was there," he said.

"Who was where?"

"At the funeral."

"Three dozen cousins. That I counted."

"Over and beyond the cousins."
"I give up. Who?"
"Enzel. Enzel was there."
"To see you?"
"Nope. To see Albert. One last look. She and Albert had a special relationship."
"Did you talk to her?"
"Sure. She's in Yreka, at a country-western club down there."
"Alone?"
"Except for Lopez."
"Who is Lopez?"
"He calls himself her manager but he's really just a general gofer."
"General Gopher?" I had images of a giant military ground squirrel.
Nikki laughed and explained the phrase. My curiosity was aroused.
"Lopez? Is he Mexican?"
"Tex-Mex. His name's Arsenio Lopez. But he's totally, I mean to-ta-lee, assimilated. I don't think he can even speak Spanish."
"Perhaps," I ventured, "she's sending you a signal."
"A signal? Of what?"
"Perhaps she wants you back."
"She'd damn well better not," Nikki said vehemently. "That's a lost cause, that is."
But if the idea alarmed him it intrigued him, too. And I could see why when I met Enzel herself later that afternoon. Nikki had driven me out to the house on the river to pick up my things and say goodbye to Phyllis. We had hardly got there when Enzel drove in in a Dodge van chauffeured by a man who looked like Pancho Villa without the bandoliers. She was gorgeous.
She was dressed in black suede from head to toe,

like a high-fashion version of Billy the Kid. She had a head full of black curly hair fluffed out in all directions and white white skin and teeth. She wore no makeup except black eye-liner. Around her waist there were crossed black gun-belts with a holster on each hip, only instead of pistols each holster carried a silver-and-ebony harmonica. It was a stunning sight. Pancho Villa stayed in the van, reading a comic book.

Enzel said hello briefly to Nikki and wordlessly gave Phyllis a long emotional hug. Then she walked around Albert's house to the riverside where in the approaching dusk the swallows were in the midst of their evening air show. She said nothing to anyone but, standing on the embankment, began to serenade Albert or his ghost. She played that old old favorite from the 1910s, "There's a Long, Long Trail A-winding"—played it in two or three different *tempi* and with amazing fugal variations. I had never before heard a harmonica played so magically.

When she had finished Nikki went over to talk to her and Phyllis and I discreetly went inside. I asked Phyllis what her plans were. She said she was putting the house up for sale and moving to Taos, New Mexico, where she had many friends.

"Write me, Agosto," she said. "I'm a good c-correspondent. And I don't stammer in my letters." She had never felt completely at home in Eugene. "I need open sky. Eugene is lovely in the summer, yes, but there's n-n-nothing but rain the rest of the year. No, no, no, I could never bear another winter here."

I took her forwarding address and promised to write— one promise I have kept; Phyllis and I are still in touch.

"There's one thing I'll never understand," she said to me. "Albert always felt the aura, always knew when something was coming before it actually happened. He must have sensed that wretched tree falling."

"Perhaps he felt it, but too late," I suggested. "After all, what could he do? It was an act of God."

She took my hands and gazed intently, in supplication, into my eyes as if her whole future life depended on my answer.

"Do you *really* think so, Agosto? That's not just a figure of speech? Is that what it was—an act of some God?"

"What else could it have been? That fir tree had been there five hundred years. The wind wasn't all that strong. Why should it fall at that precise moment?"

"Yes, yes, yes! You have to be right. There has to be a meaning to it, doesn't there?"

"I think Albert had met another magician—a *brujo* with greater powers than his."

"Yes, yes!"

"And he knew it was no use trying to escape."

"You know, Agosto, Albert used to say that he would recognize the voice of God if he ever heard it."

"What was It like?" I asked eagerly.

"Like the tide going out over a million pebbles, he said."

"Or the wind in an infinity of pine-needles?"

"Yes . . . exactly that."

"And when he heard that sound, what would he do?"

"Run and hide."

"And if there was no place to hide?"

"He didn't say. I never asked him that."

There was a long silence. Finally she kissed me on the cheek, chastely, almost like a nun saying good-bye to her relatives, and said, "Thank you, Agosto, thank you, my dear."

"I've done nothing," I protested.

"Yes. Yes, you have. You have brought me light. You have brought me peace. I can see now that it wasn't a senseless accident, no, that I couldn't bear. It was a trial of wills."

"I think so."

"And one that, ultimately, Albert knew he must lose." She went to the wall and took down one of Albert's woven hangings, one with a yellow and black mandala like a midnight sun. I saw for the first time that there was a slit across its center—it had been designed as a poncho. She bit out the threads that held it together and handed the weaving to me.

"Wear it," she said simply. "It is yours."

"It's too valuable," I said. "I couldn't possibly accept it."

"Wear it," Phyllis commanded. "Albert would have wanted it."

I slipped it over my head.

"And may its magic go with you and protect you."

Nikki came in from the patio where he had been talking with Enzel.

"We're friends again," he said.

"Oh, Nikki," his mother said, "I'm so glad!"

Nikki turned to me, plainly embarrassed by her emotion.

"Enzel has a club date in Yreka tomorrow night. She says she'll be glad to give you a lift that far south."

"I'll take it," I said.

"You've got to be ready to leave by six in the morning."

"I'm ready any time." We shook hands. "And don't take another doubles partner. I'll be back next summer to defend our title."

"Right on!" Nikki said. We all three laughed. With relief, I think.

Arsenio Lopez seemed a nervous, skittish driver. He narrowly missed a pickup truck parked by the on-ramp and even on the I-5 freeway which is four-lane from Canada to the Mexican border he steered an erratic course. He was tense and glum; I tried him in both English and Spanish and got nothing but grunts in return. Enzel sat behind us on a couch in the remodeled van practising her Irish penny-whistle, a kind of child's tin flute with a piercing tone that obviously irritated Lopez even more.

We stopped in Roseburg for breakfast which Lopez refused; he took coffee instead and then when we were ready to go excused himself and hit the bathroom. When he hadn't returned after five minutes Enzel told me to get in the car. She opened the sliding side door, pulled a duffel bag on to the sidewalk, slammed the door shut and got into the driver's seat.

"Let's go," she said and without another word nor a look back at the restaurant she drove off. Obviously, she was really mad. Of course, I wasn't about to say anything; hitch-hikers can't be too critical. Too bad for Mr. Lopez, I thought.

When we were halfway to Grants Pass she began talking.

"One hundred and one times I told that asshole no candy while you're working. Does he listen? Does he even hear me? Does he hear anybody? He's got his own crazy coked-up *Weltanschauung*. You know what that is?

"What?"

"Weltanschauung?"
"No."
"Good. I'm tired of philosophers. They're all fucked up too, only they like to give it fancy names. Do you do dope?"
"What?"
"Coke? Speed? Bennies? The noble hashish?"
"No, I don't."
"You just say no, huh?"
"I really don't know what you mean."
"Never mind. Win some, lose some. Do you have a driver's license?"
"Yes."
"Show it to me."
I did and she promptly took the Canyonville exit and parked. "You drive," she ordered. "I want to sit here and complain." We changed places and I got back on the freeway. She was silent for half an hour and then said,
"You're a better driver than he is, anyway."
"Thank you."
"What's your name?"
"Agosto."
"*You're* Nikki's doubles partner!" She said it as if she had never met me before. "You're the famous South American. Where are you going?"
"To Baja California," I said.
"Whatever for?"
"For Chele's wedding party—that's my sister. But first to San Francisco."
"No, first to Yreka."
"Right. First to Yreka."
"Why is your sister getting married? Is she a dumb Catholic girl? No offense—perhaps you're a dumb Catholic, too."

I laughed. "I'm a back-slider," I said. "And my sister is even worse—I think she's one of the eternally damned."

"Oh," Enzel said with a toss of her mop of black hair. "That's better."

There was another twenty-minute silence. Then she asked, "Shall I play my ocarina for you?" and didn't wait for an answer. "Yes, I think I will." She fumbled in her shoulder-bag and came up with what looked like a plastic sweet-potato. "What will it be, classical ocarina or old-time favorites? I know, let's do 'Sweet Betsy from Pike'—yes, I'll play 'Sweet Betsy from Pike' for you, Agosto." Which she did.

"How's that?" she asked when she had finished.

"I think I'd like it better on the harmonica."

"So do I. You show very good judgment, Agosto, I like that in you." And she played the same song over again on one of her harmonicas. She was a real virtuoso and I said so.

"Thank you, Agosto." There was another long silence, then she asked, "Where are we now?"

"Getting close to Medford."

"Stop. I want to get a case of peaches. They're in season."

We got off the freeway and found a roadside fruit stand. We sampled several of the sweet perfumed peaches of Southern Oregon, got the nectar all over our chins and finally selected a box of them and headed south again.

"You know, Agosto," Enzel said after a while, "I like you in peach-juice."

"You wear it well, too, Enzel," I answered.

We passed Ashland and began the ascent of the Siskiyou Mountains.

"I suppose Nikki has given you his version," she said out of nowhere.

"Of—?"

"Of what went wrong. Between us."

"No, he hasn't. He doesn't talk much about you. At least to me he doesn't."

"That's a point in his favor. Smoke?" She offered me a thin brown Sherman.

"No, thanks."

"I'm an addict. I'm working at getting over it, though." She inhaled deeply. "I mean it about Nikki—it's decent of him to keep quiet." Some more scenery sped past. "I hope you tennis players aren't all alike."

"In what way?"

"Smash and volley, volley and smash."

"Actually," I said, "my game is slower. Lots of lobs and spin-shots."

"That would be a relief." She looked me over appraisingly. "But I must warn you, Agosto, before you get any ideas—"

"I wasn't thinking . . ." I stammered. "I mean, I *was* thinking, but about Nikki . . . ."

She ground the Sherman out in the ashtray.

"Nikki is history," she said firmly. "Not ancient, but at least medieval. Over and done with."

"Nikki is my brother. And in South America brothers stick together. They don't touch each other's women."

"I'm not anyone's woman," she said with careful emphasis. "Only my own."

"I just wanted to make myself clear."

"You have," Enzel said. "Lucidly clear. And now let me finish my sentence. Before either or both of us gets carried away—by biology or whatever—I wanted to let you know that there are a great many things more important in my life just now than sex."

"Such as?"

"Such as my music, my job, what's wrong with the

ecology, the Indian tribes of North America, the mess in San Salvador—shall I go on?"
"No, that's enough. I think we're in California."
"I know. You have to stop here."
"What for?"
"Agricultural inspection. Don't worry, I'll take care of it."
A young, rosy-cheeked inspector approached.
"Where did you come from, folks?" he said.
"Eugene, inspector."
"Are you carrying any fruit?"
"A box of Medford peaches. With clearance."
"Any apples or citrus? Oranges, grapefruit?"
"None."
"All right." He waved us on. "Have a good day."
"That's certainly my intention," Enzel said cheerfully.
The road swooped down into the Klamath River canyon.
"All right," Enzel said and put her hand on my leg. "That's enough of history."
"No more history," I agreed, returning the gesture.
"Ancient, medieval or modern."
"*Afuero con todas las historias!*"
"This is Year One, agreed?"
"Agreed."
I stayed in Yreka with Enzel at Mrs. Anderson's Rooms for Rent for four days. Officially of course I slept in the van but Mrs. A. let me come in each morning for her celebrated pancake breakfasts. Apart from the pancakes they were four delirious sensual days and nights.
We didn't make love *all* the time; Enzel had to work at the Buckaroo Club and some mornings I worked out on the municipal tennis courts. We talked a lot, too, and learned about each other. I heard about her family in Cleveland, Ohio, where her father was a lawyer and politician, later lieutenant-governor of the state.

"My father is terrified the media will discover me," she said. "He thinks it will ruin his career. But you know, it might do him good—he's such a stuffed shirt as it is." When she was growing up she had admired his courtroom talents but when he took up conservative politics she began to feel contempt for him. Her mother she thought a nonentity—"a rabbit," was her term, "a bridge-playing rabbit." Of late she had converted to fundamentalism—"my father drove her into the arms of Jesus," is how Enzel put it—and wrote her daughter long, tearful letters pleading with her to come home.

Enzel had graduated from Oberlin and put in a year at law school before it got to be too much for her and she had walked out. Her father had offered to send her to Rochester to study the classical flute. "He could have taken it if I'd wanted to play in the Cleveland Symphony. But the mouth organ—that was too much. He thought it was a ridiculous instrument."

"Perhaps that's why you chose it," I said.

"You may be right. I certainly wanted to shock dear old Cleveland. And becoming a Country-Western musician was a sure way."

But there was still a lot of her father in her; I saw that when I watched her nightly gig at the Buckaroo Club. Once she walked through those swinging doors carefully weathered to imitate an old-time Western saloon, she changed completely. Her voice took on a brassy southern twang and she had a wisecrack and cheery smile for every ranch-hand or would-be cowboy. She sounded hard as nails—right out of West Texas, as she herself boasted. The transformation was amusing but it dismayed me, too. Why did she do it? It had taken me years of hard work learning to speak educated English and she, who had acquired the talent by birth, seemed so eager to throw it all away. Why?

"If you want to reach the people," she answered, "you have to act like one of them. They wouldn't listen to what I have to say for a minute if they thought I was a university asshole."

It was on the tip of my tongue to ask her why she would want to reach a bunch of ignorant, half-drunken cowhands, but I saw from the way her dark eyes flashed when she mentioned 'the people' that it wouldn't be smart and I kept it to myself. She set great store by 'the people' even though she was fuzzy—or so I thought—as to just who they were. Or maybe it was one of those deep cultural abysses that separate the two Americas. I, like ninety-nine percent of all Latinos, knew perfectly well that I was one of the people and put in a lot of effort trying to escape that condition, while Enzel, out of romanticism or guilt or God knows what, wanted to reverse the process and sign up with poverty and ignorance.

We talked about me, too. I was more open with Enzel than I had ever been with any woman except my sister Chele. Partly because we had agreed ahead of time that our affair was temporary and also because the sex was so direct and wonderful, I never for a moment felt I had anything either to prove or to hide with her—I was removed completely from the necessity of playing the man/woman game which we all know and practice at one time or another. I was relaxed. Which even made it easy to talk to her about my love—still very much there in the background—for Sabrina. And she wasn't jealous or judgmental, she was never judgmental as long as we kept off politics.

"Your girl sounds very lovely."

"She is."

"Of course, she's hung up. But then we all are. About something or other."

"I think she loves me. Though I'm not sure."

"No doubt part of her does."

"But which part?"

"Yes, that's the question, isn't it?" After a minute she added, more as a meditation than a considered opinion, "The other one might be better for you, Agosto."

"The other one? Which other one?"

"The one you called Vicki."

"Vicki?" The idea shocked me. "Not Vicki, no, she's totally not my type."

She kissed me on the shoulder, lazily, more in random exploration than out of any passion.

"I'm not so sure we know what our type is." She

nibbled at my skin. "I used to think I knew what it was . . . but not any more . . . ."

Sooner or later everyone gets thrown out of Eden—that's the rule of the game. In the back of my mind I expected Arsenio Lopez to show up as the snake in the garden—he was certainly the type. But he didn't. Our expulsion order came from Mrs. Anderson, the landlady, who caught us in bed together on the fourth morning. She had a 'serious and disappointed' talk with Enzel from whom she 'hadn't expected this kind of behavior.' Enzel would have to go.

Enzel stretched her lovely body and yawned.

"Fuck it," she said to no one in particular. "I'm bored with Yreka anyway."

"I'm very sad to hear you talk that way," said Mrs. Anderson aggrievedly. "You and your fiancé seemed such cultured people."

Enzel ignored her. "Help me pack," she said to me. "We're moving to Reno."

"Reno?"

"Why not? I can get a gig there. And it's on your way, isn't it?"

I didn't know whether it was or not, but I was game.

"But first," Enzel said as I drove her to the Club to collect her pay, "we're going to find Captain Jack."

"Who is he?" I was mystified.

"You'll see."

She came out of the office with Toby Paquette, a Puyallup Indian whom I knew as the Club's handyman. He was a pleasant, talkative fellow who had worked as a telephone lineman throughout California. We shook hands.

"Toby knows where the Captain is," Enzel said. "He's going to guide us."

"He keeps moving around," Mr. Paquette explained, "always one jump ahead of the Feds. The Captain's slippery as an eel. But last night I talked to a brother who met him face-to-face last Thursday and I think we can track him down. He's in the lava beds."

Mr. Paquette had an old Kawasaki motorcycle with a sidecar. We drove after him to his house to pick up his twelve-year-old son, Terry. "The kid's been dying to meet Captain Jack," he said. The boy greeted news of our expedition with whoops of glee and leapt into the sidecar.

We followed the Paquettes out of town, past the ranch village of Montague and on to the east, skirting the vast bulk of Mount Shasta, one more in the chain of great volcanoes which runs from Canada to central California. It was a clear, balmy day and the snowy peak of Shasta looked as enticing as ice cream.

"But who is Captain Jack?"

Enzel explained. Captain Jack was the last great chieftain of the Modoc Indian nation which, under his leadership, had fought and defeated a regiment of United States cavalry. Then the Captain had carried on guerrilla action for six months in the lava beds northeast of Shasta.

But all this was a long time ago?

Yes, in 1873.

Then Captain Jack would be nearly 150 years old. If he were still alive.

Yes, she admitted, it did seem improbable. Furthermore, Captain Jack was supposedly captured, tried by court martial and shot in the fall of 1873. What survived of his tribe was broken up and shipped to a reservation in the Midwest.

Then it wasn't at all likely we were going to visit the original Captain Jack?

"He was a great shaman," Enzel said.

"Yes, that might make a difference." I had respect for magic.

"And his spirit may have come to rest in another man's body."

That was always possible, I agreed.

Anyway, real or hallucination, Captain Jack had never completely vanished from Indian memory. His name was written on rocks throughout Modoc county and the messages CAPTAIN JACK LIVES! and CAPTAIN JACK WAS HERE could be found carved or spray-painted on the undertimbers of old bridges and disused mine shafts.

Now a new Captain Jack, or the old one in a new disguise, had reportedly taken up residence in the lava beds and here it was that our strangely assorted pilgrimage—Indian man and boy on a Japanese motorcycle, leather-clad *gringa* with harmonicas on her hips, and a bemused Latino traveller in a magic *poncho*—was seeking him out.

"But does he want to see us?" I asked.

"I don't know," Enzel said. "We'll have to take our chances on that."

We entered the lava beds. Toby left the asphalt and began bouncing about on a branch road built of red dirt and pulverized tufa, here and there scrawny junipers and clumps of manzanita. After a while he stopped for a consultation.

"The lava here is full of holes," he said gloomily. "There are caves half a mile long. He's here somewhere but it won't be easy to track him down. The Captain is a slippery old devil."

"Look, papá!" his son cried. "There's smoke over there!"

We stood on the raw lava staring in the direction he pointed. Neither Enzel nor I could see anything but

Terry convinced his father and we began picking our way across the blasted landscape. After about a kilometer of stumbling and leaping we all agreed there *was* a plume of smoke ahead. I expected a campfire and was amazed to see, when we came up with it, that the smoke issued from a crack in the lava; yet it was wood smoke, from someone's bonfire deep underground.

"He's here, the old devil," Toby said with a grin of satisfaction. "That's his chimney. Now we've got to find his front door."

Again it was Terry, by far the most agile of us at scrambling, who found the answer. "Papá, I've found it," he shouted. And there, concealed in a manzanita thicket, was the opening to a cave. Neatly piled by the entrance was a little store of firewood and a box of recently harvested potatoes; they seemed to be offerings left there by Captain Jack's admirers.

"Well, shall we go in?" Enzel asked.

Toby shrugged. "First we'd better erase any spells he has left here to guard the entrance."

"That's certainly prudent," I agreed.

Toby began to yowl like a wolf and his son joined in—then they chanted something in the Puyallup tongue and finally certified that the gateways had been satisfactorily cleansed. So we flicked on our electric torches and began to explore the lava tube, for that's what it was, a long pipe bringing molten rock from the hot bowels of the earth and now left, for centuries, empty by the lava's retreat. It was difficult going. In most places the tube was tall enough for one to stand but it was generally narrow and required an unpleasant amount of bending and scraping. There were also animal droppings enough to give rise to all sorts of disquieting fears of bears or bobcats. However, after a hundred meters or so it opened up into a series of chambers where we could stand up straight. In one of these rooms we encountered an Indian who seemed to be waiting for us.

"It's Captain Jack!" the boy cried.

"Sssh!" Toby answered. "It ain't the captain. No way. It's one of his guards."

The guard—if that's what he was—was dressed in dirty ranch denims and wore half a dozen vulture feathers twined in his greased black hair. He wasn't communicative. Mr. Paquette spoke to him in Puyallup which he didn't understand and then reverted to English which got a few brief answers out of him.

"It's Boston Charlie," our guide reported back. "He's one of the Captain's warriors. He says the Captain has bronchitis and isn't feeling well today."

"Will he see us?" Enzel asked eagerly.

"Maybe. But we can't stay long. And he needs money for medicine."

Enzel and I came up with a few dollars. Boston Charlie disappeared with them into the mysterious darkness.

"Wait," Toby ordered us.

"I'll bet there's bats in here," his son said.

In a minute Boston Charlie returned and signalled us to continue. We now entered a fairly large and lofty chamber stinking of wood smoke and human dung. In the center of it a low fire was burning and, surrounded by half a dozen women, an emaciated Indian man lay on a sort of deerskin cot. He looked in very poor shape, not at all like the formidable warrior who had beaten a squadron of U. S. cavalry. The women were either sleeping or keening or doing both together—they didn't seem to offer much else in support of the poor Captain who really seemed to be starving.

One by one we filed in front of the great warrior—

or his impersonator—and introduced ourselves. When it came my turn the Captain's eyes lit up and he held out his hand for me to shake. It felt like a bag of old bird wings. Then he spoke for the first time, in high, clear unaccented English.

"I know you," he said. He was very positive about it.

"Thank you," I answered politely. There was no way I was going to contradict him.

"Yes, you are Matt Kimball. Forgive me for what I did to you."

I stood there stupefied until Boston Charlie whispered, "Forgive him!" and gave me a nasty look.

So, on behalf of the absent Mr. Kimball, I forgave him for whatever might have happened.

"I know you must have suffered," Captain Jack went on. "You were stabbed as the result of bad advice, and I've regretted it for many years. I am glad to see you have recovered. You are in good health?"

"I am."

"No bothersome scars?"

"None, sir."

"And your pretty young wife from Kansas?"

"She is well, too, sir."

That seemed to comfort him, and Enzel came to my rescue by playing "Lonesome Cowboy" softly on her harmonica. Everyone—even the wailing women—fell silent to listen. When she had finished Captain Jack clapped feebly and then raised himself on his cot to speak.

"I have come here . . . on behalf of . . . the Modoc nation," he announced in what was, despite his terrible weakness, a ringing, oratorical voice . . . . "I have come here . . . on behalf of . . . justice. Perhaps I will not leave. Perhaps the gods wish me to die here. I do not know. But . . . I do not come in . . . vengeance . . . for what you palefaces have done to my people. The time for . . . vengeance . . . is past. I come for understanding . . . for justice for me . . . my . . . ."

"People," Enzel supplied since he was having obvious difficulty finishing his sentence.

"Thank you, young lady," Captain Jack said and then began coughing from the foul, smoky air in the cavern. The women rushed to his side with their handkerchiefs and Boston Charlie signalled that the interview was over. We dropped some coins in a basket and filed out through the winding, difficult lava tube. Behind us we could hear the keening echo in the caves.

When we regained the bright high-mountain sunlight I felt as if I had stepped out of a black dream. Enzel and Mr. Paquette, too, were obviously moved by the experience. Only eleven-year-old Terry was unimpressed.

"What a spook!" he said, "right out of *Poltergeist*."

His father cuffed him.

"Have some respect," he said. "The man has suffered."

In Which I Hit Bottom

Enzel and I camped that night on the eastern slopes of Mt. Lassen, the southernmost of the great chain of volcanoes which stretches from Canada to Northern California and which last erupted in 1910 and still gives off fiery vapors and hot, bubbling mud. We made love under the cold gaze of the stars and rolled about on the uneven ground so violently that we spent the rest of the night picking burrs and pine-needles out of our sleeping bags. It was a hectic night—I'm not used to camping out—and when dawn at last came we had a hurried breakfast of raisins, yogurt and icy spring water, and fled off the mountain without having much to say to one another.

Perhaps I wasn't fully awake then when I caught a sudden glimpse of some fleeting animal to the left of the road. There was a heavy bump and the van's fender began grinding against the side of the front wheel.

"Oh my God!" Enzel cried. "You've hit it!"

I stopped the car; indeed, I didn't have much choice since the bent fender almost brought us to a halt. We got out and inspected the deer, a young buck, warm but no longer breathing. It was totally dead, as Enzel would have put it if she had not been so terribly distressed. I pulled the fender back from the wheel and inspected the damage—the front left headlight was smashed but otherwise the van was all right.

But that wasn't what disturbed Enzel.

"We've got to give it a burial," she said, still seated on a tuft of frosty grass beside the dead deer.

"The coyotes will just dig it up again."

"That doesn't matter. That's *their* way; but we have the responsibility to follow *our* way." She used the word *way* as we do *sendera*, the path, the inescapable line of duty.

So we took out her fire-shovel and axe and began scrabbling a grave in the roadside ditch. It wasn't easy. The ground was rocky and compacted and it took a good two hours of hard, sweating labor before we got it deep enough for the animal's body. Even then I knew the coyotes would have it out again in half an hour. But there was no resisting Enzel when she was in one of her cosmic moods. Besides, I sensed that somehow she blamed me for the killing; indeed, from that moment I think she began to look at me with different, and more critical, eyes. I wasn't at all comfortable.

But after we had buried the deer and raised a little stone cairn over its grave, she said nothing more about it. We drove into Susanville where I had a proper breakfast while a mechanic was fixing the headlight. Enzel ate nothing but yogurt, which was a bad sign if I'd had the sense to recognize it. When we were on the road again she began playing "The Streets of Laredo" on her harmonica, very softly, while I drove through the olive-and-gray desert toward Reno. Then she returned to our meeting with Captain Jack, which seemed to haunt her.

"Weren't you afraid?" she asked.

"When?"

"When he recognized you. As a dead man."

"No. What was there to be afraid about?"

"I would have been," she said reflectively and began to play a sombre little melody that might have been a funeral march, while I thought on what it must have been like to be Matt Kimball left for dead and perhaps even scalped by Captain Jack or his warriors. But though I have a good imagination and a feeling for the dead around us, I am also pretty cheerful and can't keep my mind focused on gloomy thoughts for long.

"He's probably *loco*," I said after a while.

"Maybe."

"When I took his hand it felt like a bag of pigeon bones."

"He's a *shaman*," Enzel said as if that answered all objections. "Perhaps he's crazy, too. Many of them are. But he's still a *shaman*. I would have been afraid."

"Of what?"

"That he wasn't only seeing the past, but the future. *Shamans* get the two confused, you know."

"The boy thought he was a fraud."

"That's possible, too," she said imperturbably. "There's a lot of fraud in the best of them. But what he might have seen, Agosto, was not Matt Kimball himself but the shadow of Matt Kimball alongside you. He might have seen death travelling with you. I only say *might*."

All the same I shivered. I had suddenly seen the cracked bald skull of Dr. Laszlo Kains ahead of us in the desert and it made me tremble.

"I know," she said. "You're thinking of Albert. But that can't be it—you were a hundred miles away when Albert died; you couldn't be responsible."

I didn't tell her whom I *was* thinking of, no, nor of *El Bujo*, either, who might by now be lying dead on the back roads of Washington. Instead, I laughed and said, "We're coming into Reno."

"Yes," Enzel said. "And I have a headache."

"Well, you can't blame me for that."

She smiled sweetly. "No, it's not you. I think it must be the altitude."

I stopped at a neighborhood pharmacy to get her some aspirin. The shop was set back from the street on a pebbled walk lined with roses. An old man in cowboy boots was walking a toy poodle on the sidewalk. The druggist was eating a pork chop in the little kitchen behind the store. He wasn't at all pleased to be interrupted.

"I've got to do a wedding in ten minutes," he told me. "Are you sure you don't want Tylenol? Aspirin is bad for your stomach." I put three quarters in a row in the slot machines beside his dispensary; they all came up lemons. "Aspirin will have to do," I said.

When I got back to the sidewalk the van was gone. I asked the dog walker what had happened and he pointed down the street. There, propped against a lightpost sporting a poster advertising "The Biggest Little City on Earth," were my bag, my tennis racquets and the poncho Phyllis had bequeathed me. On top of them a note said tersely, "Thank you, Agosto." There was also a rose, lifted, no doubt, from the pharmacy garden.

"Did she say where she was going?" I asked the old man.

He shrugged. *"Ich hab kein English."* The poodle snarled and offered to bite me.

I sat down on my suitcase and began to weep. It was the most desolate moment of my life. Of course I knew things could never last with Enzel and she had told me how she hated good-byes but there was no choking back the desolation and sense of loss.

The old German stood by, sympathetically nodding and mumbling. Twelve thousand kilometers from home, exiled to a weird city of cactus and slot machines, clad in cowboy get-up and lizard-skin boots, and with an ungrateful dog on the leash, he was perhaps uniquely equipped to understand my sadness.

MYRON AND SYBIL

However, a broken heart, especially one on loan, has its way of mending, and I am by nature a *doer* rather than a *sulker*, so my season of despair lasted only for one long, sad afternoon. By that night I was determined to get out of Reno and leave all thought of Enzel as far behind as I could. So I walked through the downtown district with its gaudy circus of neon and tinsel to the bus station. As I stood deciding whether to try my luck in Sacramento where the tennis pro was an acquaintance off the circuit or head straight on for San Francisco I was approached by a friendly balding man in a three-piece suit and a polka-dot bow tie who looked like a bible salesman. He said his name was Myron, that he wholesaled shock absorbers, and shook my hand heartily. He then asked if I was, by any chance, travelling to San Francisco. I admitted that that was on my mind, at which he pressed a bus ticket on me.

"It won't leave from here," my new friend said, "but from down the street in the Rexall parking lot. At midnight. It's a chartered bus, a gamblers' special, they call it."

"And the ticket is free?"

"Absolutely, kid. Totally pre-paid. No obligation." He hesitated. "There's only one thing I'd appreciate your doing —"

"You want me to carry a package?" I asked warily, envisaging another sack of smoked salmon.

"No, nothing like that," Myron assured me. "It's the lady who'll be in the seat next to you. She's likely to be—well, just a trifle pissed, and I'd sure appreciate it, kid, if you'd . . . well, reassure her."

This seemed to be a small enough price to pay for free passage, so I agreed.

"But if she asks where you've gone, what shall I tell her?"

Myron said that Acapulco was probably his next port of call, but that I was to use my own best judgment. "The truth is, kid," he said confidentially, "something happened to me at the blackjack table. I ran ten straight bets past the dealer and then I had a revelation. No, it wasn't Jesus on the mount, not that sort. But all of a sudden I think I discovered the key to life in these here United States and I'm about to insert that key in the front door and turn it."

Very much interested, I asked him what it was.

"Mobility," he said with a broad wink. "M-O-B-I-L-I-T-Y. Money and mobility, the two Ms. Remember that, kid. When the storm-clouds gather 'round your head, just keep boogying down that road." And with another wink, he offered me a breath sweetener mint and was gone, just as swiftly as he had appeared.

I walked down the block to the chartered bus and gave the driver my ticket.

"What happened to Mister Motormouth?" he asked me.

"Who?"

"The wise guy who rode up here on the other half of this ticket."

I explained that he had sold me the ticket and taken a plane out of Reno.

"Upgrading, huh?"

"Something like that."

"Well, stow your luggage and get on now if you want to. Don't mind the bodies in the aisle. You can always tell the clients who got wiped—they get here early and go to sleep."

I thanked him and did the same, although I hadn't lost a dime, by the simple method of not risking a dime. Gambling against loaded odds has never appealed to me.

When the bus was about to pull out a large golden-haired lady smelling of perfume and whiskey plumped herself down in the seat next to me. She shook me awake.

"I'm sorry, young man," she said thickly, "but I think you have the wrong seat."

I showed her my ticket. She studied first it and then me with great deliberation. Finally she spoke.

"You are not Myron."

"No."

"And what happened to Myron?"

"He said he was sorry but he had to go to Acapulco."

"Where?"

"Acapulco. It's in the state of Guerrero. In Mexico."

"Oh." She pouted and thought this over for a while as the bus began pulling out of Reno. Then she unpinned and shook out her mop of golden hair as if its weight had interfered with her thinking. At last she returned to her slow, deliberative attack.

"You are quite quite sure?"

"That I'm not Myron? Yes, I'm positive."

"No, I can see that. I can see you are not Myron. I can see that clearly. But Acapulco? Are you sure he said Acapulco?"

"Yes, that's what he said."

"You are quite quite sure?"

"Yes."

"Oh," she said and without any warning leaned toward me and fell sound asleep, instantly, on my shoulder.

And remained there, breathing irregularly and exuding body warmth and fumes with from time to time an affectionate murmur or dream-motivated toss of her curly gold hair, through the High Sierra of California and down through the dark sentient hills where, I was aware, Captain Sutter had once toiled for gold of another sort. Only on the outskirts of Sacramento did she suddenly snap awake.

"Who the hell are you?" she asked briskly.

I told her.

"I must look a mess," she said. "And I have to be at work at eight in the morning." She seemed completely sober. "I take care of house-plants," she explained. "I do hope you didn't mind me sleeping all over you."

"Not at all," I said. "Having a beautiful woman in my arms made the trip bearable."

She gave me a nice smile for that one and then changed the subject. "Actually, it's more complicated than merely caring for them. We install the plantings for offices and restaurants, hotel lobbies and all that, and then, since no one else treats them at all well, I do the maintenance. With vitamins and a watering can. Myron is a real asshole, isn't he? It was very foolish of me to get involved with a man who is only interested in playing cards, don't you think? My hair is an utter jungle, don't you think? Look, I'm sorry about all this. My name is Sybil, what did you say yours was?"

"Agosto," I managed to get in.

"A beautiful name. I do hope you have some respect for living things. Are you a gambler? You don't look at all like one. Is it Julio? I'm terrible with names."

"Agosto. César Agosto. My mother thought I was going to be a Roman emperor."

"I knew it was one of the months. Where are we, anyway?"

"Sacramento, I think."

"A detestable place. The governor lives there. Actually, I look quite different in my overalls and watering can. You probably wouldn't recognize me. What

do you do, Agosto? Besides playing pillow, I mean?"
"I'm a tennis player."
"Well, so am I, but what do you do for a living?"
"I'm a professional tennis player."
"At your age? Really? You can't be a day over nineteen. And quite adorable, I might add. But perhaps you hate compliments? I do. They're generally so insincere. I ought to cut my hair, don't you think? It's always getting in the way."
I told her I thought it was lovely.
"Well, you ought to know, you've been practically *breathing* it all night, haven't you? But on the job it's a menace. How did you ever get Myron's ticket? Did you win it from him at poker? Myron's such an indescribable asshole, that would be just like him, to gamble me away at a card game. Did you ever see *The Girl of the Golden West*? It's by Puccini."
I confessed that I had not.
"Well, there's a poker game in it but I'm not sure how it comes out. Anyway, this is all too dreary. It's amazing how they pamper you on the way to Reno but when you've spent all your money they won't offer you so much as a drink on the way back. Where are we now? Vallejo? Another impossible place. It does sailors. Hold my hand, will you, Agosto, it's freezing outside. I can always tell when we're getting near San Francisco, the fog cuts through your bones."
Her hand seemed warm enough to me but I was past arguing. So we settled into some amiable cuddling which lasted, with time out for monologues, until we crossed the Bay Bridge and slid into foggy San Francisco. There we gradually disentangled.
"One thing I'll say for Myron," Sybil said. "He may be an utter asshole but he showed good taste in choosing you for his ticket, didn't he, darling? What a ghastly hour to be getting back. Five o'clock in the morning

and they dump you in a Safeway parking lot. I'd take you home with me, darling, but I have to be at work at eight and, besides, mother's staying at my flat with her Pomeranian. It wouldn't work, would it?"

She had a little Datsun pickup in the parking lot—it had the logo of the plant maintenance service on the door with a telephone number.

"Be a dear and copy the number down, will you? I can't see a thing without my glasses. Throw your gear in the back. I'll drop you off at a dreadful hotel I know but it's open all night and if they don't have a room they'll let you sleep in the lobby for an hour or so. Phone me soon, promise? Maybe mother will move back to Hayward and we can get together without that damned Pomeranian. It's shedding this time of the year—what a mess! I can't keep a thing clean. Here's the hotel. Don't be put off by its appearance, there's a darling Filipino man who runs it and their lobby is simply overflowing with our rental philodendrons. Mention my name. It's Sybil in case you forgot."

"I won't forget," I said as I got out. I mentioned her name at the Pitlochry and, sure enough, I got a room immediately. But I lost her phone number and never saw Sybil again.

Some Sumatran Tigers

San Francisco, as everyone knows, is a spectacular city. For several days I was content to wander it alone like the tourist I was. I also enjoyed speaking Spanish again. My hotel was in the Mission district and I was surrounded each day by thousands of South and Central Americans. There were dozens of Peruvian, Argentine, and Brazilian restaurants and meeting-places. I hadn't realized how much I had missed the sociability and excitement of a Latin city—here, at least, there was a reasonable imitation of Montevideo or Mexico, and I delighted in it. I interspersed this with a few mornings' tennis at the city courts in Golden Gate Park and in general thoroughly enjoyed my stay.

But after a week I turned to my other concerns: it was now the middle of August, I had to be in Ensenada in three weeks and, if Sabrina was coming at all to California she must be there by now. So I called the number she had given me. A woman answered with a rather clipped and cold, "Hullo, Francesca speaking," but when I explained who I was she became much more friendly.

"We've been expecting you to call. Sabrina isn't here just now but she's told us a lot about you, and Craig and I are *so* looking forward to meeting you. Where are you staying? The Pitlochry? No, I'm afraid I don't know it. But it doesn't matter—you *must* stay with us while you're in the city. Craig will be furious if you don't. Don't argue, Agosto, just bring your luggage and come along. No, no, there's plenty of room. This is a barn of a house and we knock about in it like a couple of loose billiard balls. There, that's settled, isn't it? Are you driving? No, of course not, how foolish of me to ask, you youngsters can't afford it with gas prices being what they are, can you? Well, there *is* public transportation, though I'm afraid I'll have to ask the maid to explain it to you, I don't think I've ever taken it. Hold on just a sec, will you?"

After this outpouring, all at machine-gun speed, there was a comforting pause, after which an Irish brogue explained the streetcar and bus connections; then the original voice was back:

"That *was* complicated, wasn't it? But don't worry, you can phone again if you get lost; someone will always be here, Craig doesn't believe in those hideous answering machines. Just remember, it's the last house on the right. Overlooking the sea. Number 33 Cliffside. Three-three, that's easy to remember. I'll tell you all about Sabrina's doings when you get here."

I thanked her. There was another pause.

"And by the bye, it just occurred to me, Agosto, you may not know with whom you're talking. Sabrina is invariably so mysterious, isn't she? Did she say who I am? A friend? Of course I am that, at least I hope so. This is Francesca, the Countess O'Donohu. I'm also Sabrina's mother. You didn't know? Oh, that's wonderful, that's priceless! Wait till I tell Craig, he'll be delighted, he has such a feeling for irony. Well, goodbye for now, Agosto. À *bientôt!*"

The house wasn't at all hard to find. It was a tall stone villa, walled in and with a pair of imposing stone lions on the gate posts. The district is called the Seacliff and it lies, facing the open Pacific, between the Presidio and Seal Rocks. When the sun is out the view of the Golden Gate and its approaches is truly wonderful but, as I was to find out, the sun isn't all that frequent; indeed, the area is probably consistently the most foggy and wind-swept in all of San Francisco. "Nobody in his right mind but a seagull would live out here," Robbins the man-servant confided to me on my second day at 33 Cliffside. That wasn't completely true but the district did seem to attract exiled Celtic types who longed for the damp blustery winds of their homeland. Such a one, apparently, was my host, Craigan Lockerbie O'Donohu ("no final *e*, please"), Knight of Malta, Count of the long-dead Holy Roman Empire, and Sabrina Fridley's stepfather.

When I tramped up to the house there was a limousine from the Order of Poor Clare parked in the entrance and the Countess was busy with three nuns and several swatches of knitted fabric. She shunted me off on Robbins who took my bags up to a room on the third floor overlooking the ocean. He looked askance at my tennis racquets. "They don't play much tennis out here, sir," he observed. "Too windy, too windy by far." The room had a fascinating medieval look. The bed seemed rather medieval, too, a bit like an abbot's cell, I thought, but it was definitely an improvement over the Pitlochry. I washed and went back downstairs to be received by the Countess. The nuns had gone.

"The sisters have a marvelous talent for knitting," Countess O'Donohu explained. "We've been trying to work out a line of ski-sweaters they might produce. For the profit of the Order, of course."

I said that this appeared to be an excellent idea.

"I'm so glad you think so." She seemed to mean it. "Don't you find this house a bit austere?"

No, I said, it had great style, and the simplicity that always accompanies real style.

"Thank you," she said, and again, with obvious sincerity. "There are times, perhaps only moments, when I think we may have overdone it. The simplicity, I mean."

I hastened to assure her that that wasn't the case,

and she smiled gratefully and pressed my hand.

"You're just as Sabrina said you would be, a dear boy. Of course, we're only here five months out of the year. We have a cottage in Galway and then we're in Rome a great deal on Craig's business with the Holy Father."

She made it sound as if the Pope were a member of her family, perhaps an indulgent old uncle who needed taking care of.

"And now," she continued with enthusiasm, "we must have a long, long chat about Sabrina, mustn't we? I know you're eager to hear what she's been up to. But first, you must excuse me for a moment, I have to talk to cook about dinner and order a few things over the telephone. Just make yourself quite at home, Agosto, I'll only be gone a moment." She left, toward the kitchen, but instantly popped back in again. "It's so wonderful to meet you at last, Agosto," she said. "It's such a delightful surprise. There are some magazines in Spanish in the library if you're looking for things to read." This time she was gone for good—in fact, I didn't see her again until evening prayers just before dinner. By which time I had come to the conclusion that the Countess was endearing but slightly dotty.

What Mr. O'Donohu thought on returning home to find a total stranger from Uruguay as his house guest I don't know, but presumably he was used to his wife's generosity and knew better than to fret over it. He was a large man, grave and imposing, with a well-clipt black beard and looked very much the continental investment banker and adviser of popes and *caudillos*. After vespers in their private chapel and a couple of Campari cocktails he opened up and became quite cordial to me.

"You might not guess it," he informed me, "but my ancestry is half Spanish. The other half is, of course,

Irish. But my grandfather four times removed was the Juan O'Donoju (spelled of course with the *jota* rather than the *hache*) who presented Mexico to that scoundrel Iturbide, later the short-lived Emperor Agustin I. O'Donoju, the last viceroy of Spain, the final spokesman for a lost ideal . . . ." His voice trailed off into a generalized melancholy. For all his wealth and position in the world, he was very much a lover of lost causes.

He was also a mathematician. In his library along with various coats-of-arms, he showed me one of the family treasures—not, as I had expected, some 15th-century prayer book, but a framed letter from the great physicist Albert Einstein.

"When Professor Einstein was at Princeton I had occasion to criticize some of the calculations which went into his notorious Second Law of Thermodynamics," he said in the formal, slightly pompous manner in which he always spoke. "I was not totally unqualified, since I took an advanced degree in mathematics at Yale before going into investment banking. Professor Einstein was kind enough to respond."

I studied the historic document in Einstein's own nervous slanted handwriting. To the best of my memory it read:

Dear Mr. O'Donohu:

Where you have gone wrong, I think, is in reading (here followed two lines of equations) for the somewhat simpler if less elegant (another two lines of equations).

Your (another line of equations) is most ingenious but I'm afraid here too Schrödinger has anticipated you.

Again, thank you for your so keenly expressed interest in our work.
                                         Yours,
                                         A. Einstein

"He was perfectly right of course," Mr. O'Donohu said gloomily after allowing me time to digest the document. "Theoretical physics has no place any more for amateur speculation."

The way he put it, it sounded like the passing of an age. We went into dinner where Mr. O'Donohu employed the same board-room manner in discussing with his cook the deficiencies of the chestnut dressing to the stuffed loin of pork. Everything Mr. O'Donohu touched acquired historical significance.

Naturally, that made dinner rather hard going. A conversation with him was a series of weighty pronouncements interspersed with questions by which he tried to get facts out of you with the caustic manner a prosecutor might employ with a shifty witness.

"Are you quite certain about the population of Uruguay?" he asked me (I offer one example out of many) after I had hazarded a guess. "I would have thought three million nearer the mark than five. And your chief exports—I don't really believe raw rubber is one of them. Perhaps you meant Brazil?"

And, not being Professor Einstein, I had no retort.

Meanwhile, the Countess Francesca (unlike her husband who insisted on plain Mister, she *did* like to use the title) sat for the most part in silent admiration, although from time to time she might throw in an explanatory phrase or footnote to make the workings of her husband's remarkable intellect a little clearer to the novice. It was only when she was out of the shadow of C. L. O'Donohu's overwhelming personality that she would open up; and then, just like my Auntie Lourdes of Cuernavaca when free of Uncle Sereno, a torrent of pent-up speech would burst forth.

But this evening as dinner ground toward its final fruit pudding, Mr. O'Donohu was in full charge. He had gotten onto an obviously well-rehearsed topic—the villainy of Southern California.

"Some years ago," he commenced and then, a piece of unbuttered bread aloft before him, he paused to make sure we were both at attention. "Some years ago, I say, there was a movement afoot to separate Northern from Southern California and form a 51st state. With some morsels of Oregon and Nevada thrown in, I believe. I lent that movement my name; yes, I lent it my name, although I knew of course that in the world of *Realpolitiker*, in *that* world it didn't stand a dog's chance."

"Craig has always been ahead of his time," the Countess explained.

"No, my dear," he corrected her. "Hopelessly outdated and behind my time. However," he added sardonically, "they amount to the same thing—a lack of synchronicity with the *Zeitgeist*, that's my whole predicament in a nutshell. In a nutshell, my dear."

He paused to let us appreciate the gravity of his situation, then attacked again.

"There are indeed barbarians at our gates. They have stolen our water, corrupted our religion, and given us the World of Walt Disney. Remember that, Agosto. I don't know how regular you are in your devotions—you are probably lax like so many of today's youth—but always remember that you were born into a great culture, bred to it bone and marrow, and will survive as a people only as long as you respect and nurture it."

"Craig means the Catholic faith," the Countess explained.

Again he rebuked her. "No, my dear, I mean the great entelechy of which the Faith is but one strand, however worthy. I mean the entelechy of Man's Fate and of God's design. And in that scheme of things the diabolic spirit is represented by the greed, ostentation and gross materialism of Southern California, a culture which exemplifies Protestantism in its final, most cancerously decadent state. Fortunately, there is some hope for the area now that the Mexicans are taking it over."

I could think of nothing at all to say to this. Luckily, the Irish maid came to our rescue.

"Coffee is served in the lounge," she announced.

After coffee the television was turned on to the educational channel—a nightly ritual, I was to discover. "There's a program on the Malaysian tiger Craig wants to see," the Countess said. "It should be very informative."

So we watched various leaping and stalking tigers until it got to be too much for Mr. O'Donohu.

"That's *not* the Malaysian tiger," he proclaimed angrily. "That's *tigris diversicolor*, the Sumatran tiger, an entirely different species. Any idiot with six months' training in vertebrate zoology would know the difference."

"I really don't think it's an important mistake, dear. They've probably misread the prompt-boards."

But Mr. O'Donohu was not to be soothed. "It may not be important in itself," he declared, "but it's a symptom, a symptom of too much that is wrong in our culture. The network bills itself as educational, it should live up to that billing. Laxity in nomenclature inevitably leads to sloppy thought and corrupt logic."

With a flick of his fingertip the sloppy and corrupt tigers were banished and Mr. O'Donohu marched off to his study, there to write one more letter to set things back on their proper path.

I Meet Old Friends

I was in a rowboat in the Rio de la Plata just at dawn, completely engulfed by fog. In the bow my Uncle Pablo was trying to peer through the mist with a brass telescope; behind me in the stern Sabrina sat, knitting furiously on a ski sweater. The oars were muffled with pillow casings and I knew that somewhere in the fog a pirate craft lay await to capture and torture us. We spoke in whispers. Uncle Pablo insisted that I must improve my backhand; Sabrina seemed concerned only with finishing her sweater before the entry date for some competition was closed. A great bellowing sea lion cleaved the fog and opened its vast mouth to devour us. I remember staring at its teeth and thinking that a fortune in scrimshaw lay there if only Pablo and I could harpoon it. Then I woke up.

The window was open and the cold fog swirled through it. The foghorn off Mile Rock was so loud that it seemed inside the room. My teeth ached with the cold. It was San Francisco in the middle of summer.

At the breakfast table I was alone. Blueberries, yogurt, and cornflakes were served with a coffee substitute and skimmed hot milk. The head of the house was at prayers, and when he emerged from the chapel he greeted me with a wordless nod. Silence was the order of the day at 33 Cliffside, at least before nine. Seated on a swivel-chair in his library with a towel about his neck, he allowed Robbins to trim his beard and, with a straightedge and bowl of suds, shave his bristly cheeks. Thereafter the Mercedes-Benz began growling in its pen and the time was at hand to drive

Mr. O'Donohu to that office, high in the worldly spires of Montgomery Street, where he guided the archdiocesan investments. Only then, on departure's brink, did he offer a word or two.

"The barometer, Agosto, is falling," he said. "A low pressure area is taking shape off Cape Mendocino." And with that he was gone.

Only when he was safely out of the house did the Countess emerge. When the cat's away the mice will play, I thought, and looked forward to a long chat.

"You mustn't mind Craig," she began. "That about the tigers. It was ridiculous, of course, but Craig isn't always so grumpy. I think things are going badly in Rome and, naturally, he feels the strain."

I pointed out that a man of strong convictions couldn't always control his temper and cited the example of my Uncle Pablo and his heated arguments with officials of the *Migración*.

"No," she said, "it's something that's happening in Rome. The Italians are taking advantage of the Holy Father outrageously. They've always resented him because he isn't one of them, you know."

"But why should that upset Mr. O'Donohu?"

"He's an adviser to the Papal investment office, you know." (I didn't.) "And he keeps a close eye on what they're doing with the Father's money. It's very unnerving."

"I should think so."

"Now let's have some decaffeinated and talk about Sabrina. Was your bed comfortable?"

"Oh, it was fine," I lied bravely. "Although I'll admit I hadn't expected the foghorn to be quite so close."

"After a while you think of it as an old friend," the Countess said cheerfully. "Rather like your grandfather snoring in the next room—you can't properly get to sleep without it."

"But Sabrina?" I suggested gently.

But she wasn't through with her digressions yet. "I know you must think I've been a terrible mother, Agosto."

"Not at all, Countess."

"But I have been! I can't—I shan't—deny it. To walk out on a teenage daughter, just at that trying period when she needed me the most. That's unforgivable! I know it, and I know you must think very badly of me—"

"I couldn't possibly blame you," I protested.

"Well, you should. I blame myself. I see what it has done to Sabrina. It was a sin, Agosto, a sin which only the Lord in his infinite mercy can forgive." She had talked herself into tears and now she rose, crossed the room in silence, and returned with a box of Kleenex. "You must tell me if you need more heat in your room," she said through sniffles. "Robbins can lay a wood fire in the grate. I know how draughty and cold this house can be."

"And Sabrina?" I repeated in a considerate whisper.

"Sabrina?" She sounded as though she had never heard the name before. "Oh, she was here a few weeks ago."

"And now?"

"Now, I believe she is somewhere," said the Countess with a vague wave of her hand, "in the southern hemisphere."

"South America?"

"No, no, New Zealand, I think. But she left here in such a hurry I'm not completely certain. But yes, I think she said Auckland, New Zealand. To tell the truth, Agosto, I was so upset at the time that I hardly noticed. Sabrina and Craig—well, they're both so impatient and I think they found each other . . . well, *abrasive*, if you know what I mean."

"But what is she doing in New Zealand?"

"For the life of me I couldn't say." She dabbed at her eyes with a bit of Kleenex. "I think you'd better ask her friend Victoria. She hears from Sabrina all the time."

"Vicki? Her Seattle friend?"

"You know her?" I detected a certain edge of resentment in her voice. "Yes, she *was* from Seattle but she's down here now. Just across the bridge in Sausalito. She's working for some frightfully successful developer with extremely poor manners. His name is Wilder Fawcett—you couldn't forget that name, could you? It's so utterly bizarre. I think Victoria is selling vacation homes, which I suppose is vaguely useful, though that sort of thing is quite out of my world. Yes, Wilder Fawcett, that's the man's name though I've never been quite sure precisely what he sells. Would you like to see her?"

I thought it over a moment and said yes.

Which is how I came, a day or so later, to have luncheon at the Café Con Gusto in Sausalito.

Vicki looked great. Divorce definitely agreed with her. "Thank God for the judicial system," she said over her *tortellini al pesto*. "It has started many a poor girl on the path to a new life." She still wore too much lavender eye make-up but here in the brassy California sunlight (the fog had cleared) it seemed to have been acclimatized. Or perhaps I had changed. Anyway, for the first time I found myself admiring her self-possession and cheerful, aggressive good humor.

We sat under a grape arbor on an abrupt hillside with San Francisco and its bay spread out before us. It was dotted with wavelets and white triangles and looked remarkably like one of those paintings of the Bay of

Naples which decorate the walls of every last Italian *trattoria.*
"Gusti, you must meet Wilder," she was saying. "You'd love him. He's an ex-slalom champion with a sense of humor. And vision. He's going to make millions. And without being in the least bit stuffy about it."
"I hope he's not another Dr. Kains."
"That's a brutal blow, Gusti. You're hitting under the belt."
"It's just a friendly warning."
"I know, I know. My judgment hasn't always been perfect. In fact, the more I think of it, the worse it looks to me. Poor Laszlo! Did he suffer much?"
"I didn't stay around to find out," I said. "It looked instantaneous to me."
"I hope so. But Wilder is totally different. He doesn't even smoke grass, for God's sake!"
"Why didn't you come that day?"
"Oh, that was Sabrina's idea, not mine. I was gung-ho for a flight. But Sabrina got cold feet."
"She said you had a migraine headache."
Vicki laughed. "Sabrina always says that when she doesn't want to do something. 'Vicki has a headache and I have to take care of her.' It's an old ploy with her."
Here the wind suddenly sprang up and almost blew away our checkered table cloth.
"Oops!" Vicki cried. "There goes the vinegar bottle."
We retrieved the wandering vinegar cruet and then Vicki turned serious.
"She loves you, Gusti, I know she does. It's just that she can't face any commitment now. She's frightened, so her response is to run away somewhere. Of course it's cowardly, but I understand it."
"But why New Zealand?"

"Didn't Francesca tell you?"

"She did everything she could to avoid telling me anything."

"That's because she's furious with Sabrina. She was supposed to spend August here in San Francisco with the family. But she can't stand His Imperial Highness O'Donohu, so she went to the South Pacific instead."

"But why New Zealand?" I repeated.

"It has something to do with stopping the Japanese whaling fleet. In the Antarctic, I think. Didn't she write you?"

"How could she? I had no address."

"Well, I know she meant to. She's joined Greenpeace. The ecology movement." She saw my crestfallen look. "Honest, Gusti, I tried to talk her out of it. But she said she had to find her identity before she would be good for you or anyone else. I know that's a *cliché*, but I think she really means it. She's been looking for something to identify with for as long as I've known her, and it couldn't be religion after she saw what *that* had done to her mother."

"Did she say when she was coming back?"

"No. But you know Sabrina. Some day she'll pop up again, saved or not saved, what's the difference? We'll go on just as we did before. Sabrina is like that. But Gusti—"

"Yes?"

"I wouldn't be waiting for her. If I were you, I mean."

I was hurt but I covered it up with a laugh.

"I can't anyway," I said. "I've got to be at my sister's wedding. If we meet again it's going to be in South America."

"I wouldn't put that past her," Vicki said.

We split the check and went our separate ways, leaving the napkins to swirl wildly over the patio. The wind

always comes up in the afternoon in Sausalito.
 The next morning I rode downtown with Robbins and Mr. O'Donohu and called on the Uruguayan consulate. I had been given a grant by the Tennis Federation to cover my expenses on the Japanese trip and the final check had not come through. Naturally, the consul knew nothing about it but he very politely promised to make inquiries and let me know what had happened. Afterwards, I found myself on Sutter Street not far from the address Mr. Wetherall had given me, and it occurred to me that it was time to see how Plains of Plenty was doing.
 The office of Imperial Consolidated was there all right, on the fifth floor of a building mainly tenanted by lawyers and collection agencies. The reception room displayed a Mexican roping saddle heavily decorated with silver studs, and on the walls were *sarapes* and hand-tooled belts from Chihuahua and Durango. A very pretty receptionist informed me that, yes, Mr. Wetherall was in San Francisco but, no, he wasn't in today and she thought he was golfing somewhere. He came and went, she said. And, as if to substantiate that opinion, just as I was leaving who should pop in but Mr. Wetherall himself, more sunburned than ever and apparently not too pleased to see me. However, once over the initial shock, he took me into his private office which I thought a bit cramped for a multi-millionaire investor and offered me a cigar and a glass of whiskey, both of which I declined.
 "Well, young feller," he said rather grimly. "I think you might say the shit has hit the fan."
 I asked him what he meant by that metaphor.
 "Feathers and fur are flying," he said and downed his whiskey at a gulp. "The IRS has just disallowed every last limited partnership our deceased friend syn-

dicated. Poor old Albert. He was too smart for them while he was alive, so now he's dead and can't defend himself the bastards are out to smear him."

"That seems very unfair."

"Young feller, we are dealing with people who don't even know the meaning of the word *fair*. But never mind the dead for a minute. We the living are in deep shit, too."

I asked him how that could be.

"Our names are on a lot of those investment trusts as officers, that's how."

"*My* name?" I was astounded.

"I'm afraid so. You're down for the South American cattle syndications."

"But how could it be?" I protested. "I only joined the board a month ago."

"A lot of the syndications were pre-sold. The names were filled in afterwards. It's done all the time." He saw my dismay and tried to console me. "But why should you worry, young feller? They can't get into you for anything because you haven't got it." He poured himself another straight shot. "On the other hand, I stand to lose a golden piss-pot if this ain't straightened out. The investors have just lost millions in tax exemptions—they're going to come after me in spades."

I asked him if there was anything I could do to help him over these difficult days.

"Just keep a low profile," he advised me. "And never, under any circumstances, talk to the IRS without there's a lawyer in the room. If they call on you, you call this number." He handed me an attorney's card. "Get it?"

I said I got it.

"One other thing: It's not only the Feds. Some of the syndicating partners are pretty big guns and when I say *guns* it ain't a figure of speech. There's some rough hardware involved in this. They lose money and they're hot to trot. Bang, bang, and ask questions later. Get it? No reason for alarm, but caution is called for. Need any money?"

I said there was no emergency. He gave me $500 in cash just the same.

"You might as well get some while it's still here," he said with a wry laugh. "Next month, who knows? Have Sally write you a travel voucher. Everything has to be in the books. Some of the auditors they send round these days can even read."

I thanked him and promised to check back in a week.

"No," he said. "Keep away from this office. Give me your address and I'll get in touch with you."

I gave him the O'Donohus' address which he wrote down in his pocket notebook. Of course, if I had guessed that I wasn't going to see him again, ever, I would have been more careful about the address, but at the time I only thought he looked flushed and not at all as healthy as one would expect from all the golf he played.

A Roman Tragedy

I had been at 33 Cliffside for only four days but had already broken all my previous records for prayer attendance and, as the Countess had foreseen, I was beginning to become attached to the foghorns when my new life as a devotee was suddenly up-ended. I returned from a morning run through the Presidio to find the house in turmoil—the servants running from floor to floor with luggage and clothing and the Countess in a state of nervous hysteria.

"Oh, Agosto!" she cried as I walked in the door. "I'm dreadfully afraid I'm going to have to uninvite you. We're closing up the house and flying to Rome tonight. It's a simply frightful emergency. Pack your things. If you go right now I can let you have Robbins and the Mercedes—we don't have to be at the airport until five. I'm dreadfully sorry, Agosto, I had so looked forward to long talks with you about Sabrina, and now they'll have to wait for another time. Hilda! Hilda!"

"Yes, ma'am?" the maid answered from the landing above.

"Did you phone the Pitlochrie about Mr. Villaseñor?"

"I did, ma'am," came the shouted return. "They say he can have his old room back."

"There. You see," said the Countess triumphantly. "There is no problem. But you must hurry. Robbins will help you with your luggage."

"But what has happened?"

"It's the most dreadful tragedy. I really don't have the time to explain it all. Hilda!"

"Yes, ma'am?"

"I *must* have anything in black that's presentable.

It's been on the television all morning. Frasconi has failed and Mr. Crivelli has killed himself. In the bank's boardroom, of all places! There were hideous pictures of the body simply *sprawled* on the bloody parquetry." Her eyes flashed and her hair was disarrayed; suddenly, in the depths of tragedy, she looked very much like her beautiful daughter.

"Frasconi? Crivelli? Who are they?" My head was in a spin.

"The Italians! The Italians!" the Countess cried, as if that explained and justified everything. Then, seeing that I was still mystified, went on: "They managed the Holy Father's banking and now they've cheated him out of millions! And Crivelli dares to commit suicide in the Vatican, too—a mortal sin! Craig warned the Holy Father not to trust Frasconi. They pretended to be so pious and it was all a sham. And now he has to drop everything and fly to Rome to help straighten the mess out. Imagine! They were gambling with His Holiness's money. It's all on the television. They were connected with some racketeers from . . . Southern California!"

I scarcely heard these last sentences because I was suddenly convinced that it was Sabrina there in front of me, inexplicably returned from New Zealand. I don't know what brought that on, but it was more than a random impression, it had the force of absolute reality. And my response was to put my arm around the Countess to comfort her; for a moment I felt her warm agitated body next to mine.

"I'll go with you to the airport," I said. "I wouldn't think of leaving you. Not now. Not when I can be of help."

I felt her body stiffen.

"You take a great deal for granted, young man," she

said icily. As if I had touched a secret spring, she tore herself away from me and, in an instant, all the anger she had felt toward the recreant Crivelli was hurled at me.

"What right have you to reproach me? You think I walked out on her, don't you? That's what you meant. Of course you're not honest enough to come right out and say it, but that's what you meant. That innocent air doesn't fool me. I know a hypocrite when I see one. Not only that, you're a meddler, too. What goes on between my daughter and me is a family affair and no concern of yours. We don't need your meddling, get that straight!"

Naturally, I was mortified by her onslaught, provoked by what I meant as a simple gesture of sympathy, but I was also tongue-tied in the face of this avalanche of accusation.

"Ever since you came here you've been spying," she went on implacably. "Trying to find out things Sabrina didn't choose to tell you. You're a little sneak, that's what you are, so polite on the surface and all deviousness inside. Perhaps you thought you could turn me against Sabrina—is that it? Well, it won't work—nothing can separate us, nothing! I can see now why Sabrina was so afraid of you."

But that was enough—I wasn't going to play her game any more.

"Thank you, Countess, for being frank," I said in my most formal manner. "I think it's obvious I have overstayed my welcome." I bowed and walked quickly upstairs to pack.

But when, ten minutes later, I came down with my bags, everything had turned around. The countess was weeping; she rushed to the stairway to throw her arms around me. "Forgive me, Agosto," she cried and threw herself down like one of the *penitentes* before the Virgin of Guadalupe. "I'm so horrible! You must forgive me! No, no, you can't go now! You must wait till Craig gets here, he wants to talk to you. He thinks of you like a son! I'm so detestable, I have such a burden of shame! You have no idea how I suffer. Please, please, Agosto, say you forgive me."

What could I do? I forgave her, she kissed me, and in a few moments, such is the restorative power of compassion, she was laughing and joking with me as we helped the maid pack her things. Dotty but endearing had been my capsule opinion of the Countess O'Donohu when we first met; now, I was inclined to emend it to dotty but dangerous.

With C. L. O'Donohu, however, crises merely provoked his executive talents; like his ancestor, the redoubtable Juan O'Donoju, he was thoroughly at home amidst collapsing empires and when he showed up at 33 Cliffside order and tranquillity were at once restored. "My dear," he informed his wife, "Hannibal took forty-eight days to cross the Alps from France into Italy. Thanks to modern physical research we are able to accomplish one hundred times that in the passage of an evening." She seemed greatly calmed. Buttermilk was served all around and the Count took warm leave of his servants, among whom, unaccountably, he seemed to place me. I suspected that, in the rush of the day's melodramatic events, he had forgotten who I was. How else explain the pair of tickets he pressed on me, tickets to a lecture by Father Emil Finnerty, S. J., on *Historic Wines of Apulia*? "Finnerty is a remarkably distinguished enologist," he informed me. "You can profit from his *expertise*."

I bowed and assured him I would attend with pleasure. I felt exactly as my father must have when confronted by Mr. Hyatt.

I went with them to the airport, then, seated up front with Robbins. The Countess kept gazing at me with the contrite air of a child caught stealing sweets; her husband, a calculator on his lap, was already guiding the Holy Father through a labyrinth of deficits. Neither spoke.

After they had gone Robbins drove me to the Hotel Pitlochrie where I created a small neighborhood sensation by arriving at that rather *déclassé* establishment in a chauffeured Mercedes. As for Robbins, he smiled wryly as he unloaded my racquet cases.

"I warned you, sir," he said. "You wouldn't get much chance for tennis out there."

A Tempting Offer

Nothing more held me in San Francisco and, although the Filipino owners of the Pitlochrie were the souls of kindness and understanding, I had grown sick of that cramped hostelry and its lobby full of diseased philodendrons. September was approaching and it was obviously time for me to make my way to Ensenada and the wedding party. But as I was on the verge of departure for the bus depot I got a call from Vicki who insisted that I delay leaving until her employer, Mr. Wilder Fawcett, had a talk with me.

"I think he has a job for you, Gusti."

"But that's impossible. I have to be in Mexico in three weeks and, anyway, I can't work on a tourist visa. Once I've gone they'll never let me back in."

"Wilder understands that. And he has a million and one connections. He can get you a green card with a single phone call. Don't go until he talks to you." There was a pause. "Look, we're driving up to the Napa Valley tomorrow to check out a hot air balloon he's buying. Come with us. We'll pick you up at your hotel."

"All right. As long as I don't have to go up in it."

She laughed. "It's not obligatory. But you might love it."

"I doubt that."

"Don't knock it if you haven't tried it."

So early next morning Vicki and Mr. Fawcett picked me up in his Bentley, creating another sensation at the hotel; by now I was sure they thought me a South American ambassador at the very least.

On first meeting Wilder Fawcett one noticed his white

teeth and heavy tan; he wore a canary-yellow silk jacket and several gold chains but the tan was what caught my eye. In Mexico the well-to-do scrupulously avoid tans; if asked, they talk about the dangers of skin cancer, but everyone knows that the real reason is that they're afraid of being taken for Indians. In the United States, on the other hand, there aren't many Indians around, so it is fashionable to look like one. A heavy tan is also evidence that you've been somewhere tropical and expensive; in Mr. Fawcett's case his T-shirt let you know it was Maui.

He was very cordial to me and was quite unlike any salesman I had hitherto met—indeed, with his shock of graying curly hair he looked more like an off-duty symphony conductor than a businessman. Mr. Fawcett's ruling passion was something known as *time-sharing*. As we drove across the Golden Gate Bridge and headed north toward the Napa Valley he explained, in a vibrant baritone, the philosophy underlying this practice.

"Start with a clock," he began. "Consider it—that watchman of mortality, as Byron or Pushkin or someone in that line of work once said. When you're having a good time you don't give Time a thought. Then the clock shows up—just an ordinary, run-of-the-mill clock, an insipid disk with a painted face and greedy little hands. Bingo! One glimpse of it and enjoyment is gone, like smoke in the wind. You yawn, you're bored, you start thinking of death—"

"Perhaps we should outlaw clocks," Vicki suggested.

"Treating a symptom won't cure the disease. No, Time-Fear is too deeply embedded in the Western subconscious for that to help. Boredom is merely a symptom of Time-Fear. And I'm afraid there is no eliminating that. The best we can do is to spread it around, so that no one person has to carry more than his fair share. That is, of course," he concluded, "the psychological basis for all time-share programs."

He paused to make sure we had digested this. The Bentley purred through the golden, unreflecting hills of Marin County.

"I see," I said.

"Yes," said Vicki. "Yes."

"Merely as an example, let's consider our condominium complex on Maui. It's across a busy highway from the nearest beach, stuck between a 24-hour sushi bar and a carpet outlet; the lawn is minimal Bermuda grass, the swimming pool generally drained; the night life is totally alcoholic and there is no discernible surf. Buying one of these condos with the intention of living there year-round would be an act of insanity, probably certifiable. However, for a little over $10,000—a sum you will hardly miss—we can sell you one week each year for the rest of your natural life, just one week of exciting boredom at the more-or-less edge of the sea. We are prepared to guarantee the water temperature."

We sat in silence, numbed by the flow and force of his rhetoric.

"It's advertised as *Your Week in Paradise*. That's safe enough; everyone expects boredom in paradise—the church has taught us that."

"You have me convinced, Wilder," Vicki laughed. "If I had ten thousand free I'd sign up. But I think you'd better slow down a bit. There's a quite obstreperous police car behind that wants us to move over."

In his enthusiasm Mr. Fawcett had been driving at around 130 km.p.h. He now responded to the flashing lights and siren by pulling off on the shoulder and purchasing two tickets to a charitable dance for the widows of patrolmen killed in the line of duty, after which we were sent on our way with much friendly waving, in which even I joined. I couldn't get over how polite the American police are.

"Sure," Mr. Fawcett agreed. "All over the world money grins, doesn't it?"

We stopped for coffee and pastries in Yountville.

"I can see you're a fine lad, Agosto." Mr. Fawcett gave me a gleaming, encouraging smile.

"Thank you, sir."

"And Victoria tells me you are a top-flight tennis player."

"Who?"

"Me," said Vicki. "That's me. Victoria-Evangeline Moore."

"Well, sir," I explained. "I'm actually quite a way from the top. The very top, that is."

"Gusti is the Oregon state champion," Vicki said.

"Only in doubles, sir."

"*Oregon title-holder*," said Mr. Fawcett. "That has a ring to it. It rolls on the tongue. People respect Oregon. It suggests tall timber and honest cheese. Now if it were *Nevada champion*, that suggests flashiness, something a bit off-color."

"And Idaho?" I wanted to watch his mind at work.

"Strictly the boondocks. Where Hemingway shot himself. No pizzazz, only potatoes. Almost as bad as Dakota. Who would pay money to work with the champion of South Dakota? No way. But Oregon title-holder—that might cut the mustard." He sighed. "Of course, California would be better."

"I doubt if I'm good enough for that, sir."

"We could stage our own tournament," Mr. Fawcett reflected. "And limit entries to the bozos you could handle. But I suppose that might be unethical."

"Yes, Wilder, it definitely would."

"A pity."

"Gusti has world ranking."

"Mr. Fawcett's teeth lit up. "World ranking! That's the hook! Never mind the Oregon title. *Study with a world-class professional!* That should bring them in."

"Bring them in where?" I asked.

"Drink up," Mr. Fawcett commanded. "I'm paying." He rose from the counter, impatient to be off and confront the next hurdle. I gulped the last of my coffee while Vicki (now looking more and more like Victoria-Evangeline) explained that Mr. Fawcett had me in mind as the resident tennis professional at his time-share complex at Dinosaur Mountain in the southern Sierra.

I said the idea was tempting but once again explained my problems with the immigration people. Mr. Fawcett was not dismayed; as I was to learn, no difficulty ever dismayed Mr. Fawcett.

"So? So, you won't go on the official payroll until I can get you a green card. No problem. In the meantime you can have free rent and commissions—"

"Commissions?"

"Well, naturally, Agosto, you would be expected to dabble a bit in sales. At least until the tennis players showed up. This will be a new program: ski instruction in the winter—I'd handle that myself—and tennis in the summer; a balanced all-round program of wholesome family entertainment."

"But, sir," I objected, "the summer is nearly over."

"Yes, I'd noticed that," he said drily. "That's why you'd have to concentrate your efforts in sales to begin with." He must have seen my hesitation, for he suddenly turned jovial. "Of course you wouldn't actually do the sales. The closers do that. You'd just be making introductions. Friend to friend. Introducing is great sport, Agosto, we all enjoy that more than any other part of the game. Introducing, that's the pearl in the oyster. Opening the door of opportunity for some poor klutz who has never known what leisure living can be like. We all enjoy introductions the most, don't we, Victoria?"

Vicki agreed. "A gas," she said. "Once you get used to it, a positive gas."

"We'd love to have you on board," her employer said warmly. "Give it a try, Agosto. Of course, you can have time off for your sister's wedding. Things are slow just after Labor Day anyway."

I thanked him for his kind offer and asked for a day to think it over. Actually, I had no intention of going to work for him, although events were soon enough to change my mind.

UP IN THE AIR

The day was an absolute joy. We had left the fog behind and the air was windless and sparkling. Hectares of vines, heavy with soon-to-be-harvested grapes, crowded around us and the hills were dotted with pink-and-cream villas and an occasional mock castle. It was like a child's garden of delight; I felt wonderfully soothed and content.

Just south of Calistoga we drove onto the field where the balloons were kept, amazing brightly-striped pears of nylon with wickerwork baskets attached.

"Every new time-share owner," Mr. Fawcett said proudly, "is going to receive a complimentary champagne flight for the whole family; Rover, too, if they can persuade him to get into the basket."

"Wilder has these simply incredible promotional ideas," Vicki said.

"The name of the game," said Mr. Fawcett.

We were introduced to Edgar who prepared the balloons for ascent, a gloomy-looking man in a blue jumpsuit and drooping moustache.

"She's ready for you," Edgar said. "I've got the burners on low. She's acting a bit cranky this morning, but not to worry, once she gets out of the stable she'll go up like a ball of smoke."

This didn't reassure me; apparently Edgar thought of his charges as wayward mares poised for a gallop. But Mr. Fawcett approached his steed cheerfully, a picnic basket on his arm and a checkered tablecloth over his shoulder. "We'll have lunch in the air," he announced. "I've brought a *pollo asado* and a couple of bottles of

Chardonnay."

I began to shiver. Apparently they took it for granted that I was going to accompany them in the purple-and-white balloon which now stood, propane burners whispering softly, at the ready. Nothing was further from my mind.

Here I ought to say that under normal circumstances I might have loved the challenge—I have flown a lot in conventional planes and until now had never been reluctant to take to the air. But since my ill-fated flight with Dr. Kains something had changed within me. I had definitely lost my nerve. And, what was worse, as I stared at the nylon balloon, I saw in its place the professor's bald egg-shaped skull, down to the purple bruise and the drops of blood. It was definitely a bad omen.

Mr. Fawcett held the door to the basket open as Vicki jumped up into it. There was a brass plate with the balloon's name on it: *Icarus II*. That did it. I ran hastily back to the car.

"Hurry up, Gusti!" Vicki called.

"I left my sarape," I shouted. "It's here some place."

Once out of sight behind the Bentley I thought for a moment I was going to vomit. The day had suddenly turned terrifying.

"The heat's turned up!" Mr. Fawcett cried. "We've got to go."

The *Icarus II* tugged impatiently at its tethers; obviously it wanted to be off.

"I'm coming!" I shouted and ran toward it, managing with considerable cunning to catch my foot in one of the ropes and fall sprawling to the ground. I yelled ferociously and Edgar ran to my side to help me up.

"I think I've sprained my ankle." I limped over to

the basket where Vicki and Mr. Fawcett leaned out a few feet above my head. "I'd better get it taped, it's bound to swell."

"I could tape it for you," Vicki said. "I used to tape Rob's knees every time he tried to play basketball."

"No, no, it won't need it," I said hastily. "The best thing is just to keep off it for a while." And to Mr. Fawcett I added, "I'm afraid, sir, the altitude won't be good for it. It will increase the swelling."

"All right," said Mr. Fawcett dubiously. "We'll have to leave you behind."

"I'm afraid so."

He dropped me his car keys.

"Sit in the Bentley. We'll be back in half an hour. If you get bored there are some cassettes on sales technique in the glove compartment."

And they cast off the mooring ropes and began to ascend without me. The burners, turned full up, roared their delight and the purple-and-white envelope was soon far overhead.

And then a magical thing happened. The bowl of the sky, which up to then had been so still and crystalline, broke into splinters. A wind came up out of nowhere, leaves, twigs and bits of paper swirled over the bare landing field, and an octet of blueblack clouds, round as bowling balls, appeared over the valley's southern rim and began rolling toward us. The *Icarus II*, which a second before had been directly overhead, swayed back and forth as if in momentary indecision, then scudded briskly to the northeast.

"That's a nasty williwaw," Edgar observed. "They come up like that. Usually later in the afternoon."

I didn't tell him that it came as no surprise to me; in a way I felt that I had foreseen it.

"I've got some liniment for your ankle." He took a

flask from his coveralls. "You can pour it on your foot if you want to but that'd sure be a waste of good whiskey."

I felt obliged to take a drink. It scalded my throat; if I took enough of it I felt sure it would blind me. The balloon was now rapidly becoming a mere dot on the horizon.

"Not to worry." Edgar was gulping from the flask. "She'll come down somewhere. She's got gas for five hours. Lucky the wind ain't blowing toward the sea. It's mighty damp out there."

Since he didn't seem alarmed, I made a show of limping to the car, got in and closed the windows against the stiff wind which was now slapping at the nylon of the tethered balloons. After a while Edgar gave up on the day's flying and started folding and stowing them in his shed. I sat in the Bentley and meditated on the fate which had brought me here and so abruptly snatched my companions away. I wasn't in any mood to listen to Mr. Fawcett's sales tapes.

Sitting there in the Bentley, with Vicki and Mr. Fawcett blown out of control over the Napa mountains, I began to wonder if Enzel hadn't been right when she said I might be the carrier of a curse. It certainly looked as though most of the people I met in North America were married to disaster. Why? Did I bring it with me? My Aunt Serena of Cuernavaca used to talk a lot about people who were turned into birds and then showed up, cawing or screeching, at the nearest funeral. You could even predict death, she claimed, by the appearance of crows above a house, or albatrosses over a ship where someone lay sick. Was I an albatross? Either in this life or a previous one? Or was I, all unconsciously, a Jonah in the belly of a whale as large as a continent? The evidence against me was certainly piling up.

Of course it *was* possible that the fault wasn't mine at all, that the deaths and misfortunes which seemed to follow me were typical of life in North America. Perhaps the citizens there were continually walking a frayed rope over the gulf of disaster. But that didn't seem too likely. I have talked with many South Americans who have toured the North; they all spoke of the Grand Canyon, Disneyland, Yosemite, the American hamburger with all its relishes, Las Vegas, Knott's Berry Farm and quaint old Carmel-by-the Sea. Some commented on the swift freeways, others on the relaxed American manners and the size of the gourds. But no one reported experiences like mine. We seemed to have travelled in entirely different countries. Who else had shovelled Purina to sixty howling beagles? Smuggled smoked salmon?

Called on the illustrious Captain Jack in a lava cave? Become a *prestanombre* on a corporate board of directors? Been the houseguest of a Papal count? No, simply asking such questions makes plain the unique and sinister nature of my travels.

But if I was Jonah, what could I possibly do about it? I sighed. And then sighed again. There is a Spanish proverb that says that the crow can trade away his feathers but no other bird will take his soul. I felt very much like that crow.

After a couple of hours of waiting I put Albert Holiwell's magic *sarape* on and, to Edgar's amusement, chanted a bit. It wasn't exactly a prayer but I thought anything I could do for Vicki's safe return wouldn't be wasted. Finally, at around five that afternoon a dusty old pickup drove onto the field. Mr. Fawcett was at the wheel and Vicki was bouncing around in back as she tried to keep the collapsed balloon under control. They had come down in the middle of Lake Berryessa, some fifty kilometers away and had been hauled out of the water by startled fishermen.

"I thought we were going to drown," Vicki said proudly. "But Wilder was marvelous—he wanted to swim out with me on his back. Everything is soaking wet, of course, and we lost the two bottles of wine. But I brought a piece of the chicken back for you, Gusti, I knew you'd be simply starving."

As for Mr. Fawcett, his canary-yellow jacket was utterly ruined and he had lost one shoe in the lake, but there was no dampening his jubilation.

"It was like being in touch with a new life," he exulted. "Half a mile up and not a sound. Only you and the wind. I know now how the astronauts must feel." Drifting aloft in the *Icarus II* before its plunge a splendid new idea had come to him. "From Maine to California, what is it every red-blooded American youngster dreams of?" he asked rhetorically.

"Masturbation," Vicki said brightly.

"Cut the cynicism, Victoria. The answer is—*owning a circus*. Being the boss of lions, elephants, trapeze artists, the whole schmeer, even a set of baggy-pants clowns in size 21 Reeboks. And I'm going to make that possible! I'm going to make that dream come true for every family with $15,000 to spare. Mr. and Mrs. Middle America are going to have their very own private circus for one week out of every year for the rest of their lives. I'll buy one and syndicate it. Time-sharing is going to open the door to excitement for Dick and Jane. Think of that!"

"That's tremendous, Wilder," Vicki said and added, "You'd think they'd have a Ladies Room around here somewhere. It's been a hell of a long day."

While she went in search of it Mr. Fawcett and I helped Edgar fold and store the balloon.

"*Ringmaster for a Week*. How does that sound for a slogan, Agosto? Would that tempt you?"

"It certainly would, sir," I said. "I hope there will be bareback riders—I like them particularly."

Edgar said nothing. I don't think he enjoyed being kept overtime.

"The swelling is better," Vicki said after inspecting my ankle. "But I'm going to tape it anyway."

"I guess it was only a strain," I said weakly. Actually, I had even forgotten my limp.

"No protests, Gusti. These things can turn nasty if they're not taken care of."

"You'd better do as Victoria says, young man," Mr. Fawcett said with an avuncular smile. "She generally knows best."

So in Napa we bought an elastic bandage and Vicki bound up my unprotesting foot as we drove down the east shore of San Francisco Bay. In Berkeley we stopped for crab sandwiches. Mr. Fawcett bought a paper for the football scores—I gathered he had money riding on the results—and passed the front sections to Vicki and me. A headline caught my eye.

IMPORTER FOUND SLAIN IN PARKING LOT

The story beneath began, "In what police termed a gang-land execution, the body of William Poindexter Wetherall, 62, well-known importer and president of Bay States Shrimp Farms Inc., was found yesterday crammed into the trunk of a rented limousine in the long-term parking lot at the S. F. Airport. He had been shot twice at close range in the back of the head—"

I must have shivered and turned pale because Vicki asked with concern, "What's the matter, Gusti? Is it your ankle?"

"No, it's n-nothing," I stammered.

But she had seen the story.

"Did you know him?"

"He was an . . . acquaintance."

"Look, Wilder," she said, waving the paper. "Gusti has a friend who has just been blown away!"

Mr. Fawcett's mouth was stuffed with shreds of lettuce and crustacean. "Happens every day," he managed.

"He wasn't a friend," I protested. "Just someone I met once or twice . . . in Oregon."

"Still, it must be a shock."

"Yes, of course."

"Was he a gangster?"

"Not that I knew of."

"Let me see," said Mr. Fawcett, finally free of his sandwich. "Hmmm. It says here the police found membership cards to nineteen different golf clubs on the body."

"Yes," I said. "He was into golf."

When they dropped me off at the Pitlochrie I was in for another surprise. As Heriberto, the night clerk, gave me my key he announced that I had had a caller that afternoon. He passed me a business card. It was from Philip S. Fogarty, an attorney; on the back Mr. Fogarty had scribbled, "Plains of Plenty Shareholders Assoc.— call me A.S.A.P."

"Thank you, Heriberto," I said. "What did this Mr. Fogarty look like?"

"I wasn't on duty when he came in. But we had to get out the carpet-sweeper after he left. He was spitting sunflower seeds. Not a gentleman, I think, Mr. Agosto, not a gentleman."

"Thank you, Heriberto. If you'll make up my bill I think I'm checking out. Early tomorrow."

He said the hotel would be sorry to see me leave but added sympathetically, "I myself personally have had problems with the telephone company for several years. Would you like a wake-up call?"

"At five o'clock, please."

I got a few hours of fitful sleep and was on the first bus south in the morning. At eight-thirty I was in Fresno and found a pay phone and called Vicki. I think I woke her up because she had a hard time comprehending where I was.

"Fresno? What in God's name are you doing there?"

"I've thought it over," I countered. "Tell Mr. Fawcett I want to accept his offer."

"That's wonderful. But the development isn't in Fresno, Gusti." There was a pause, then I heard her say to someone else, "It's Gusti. He's lost." In an instant she was back with me. "Wilder is here—he just came by to take me to work—and he's delighted. Aren't you Wilder?" Apparently he was, for Vicki now proceeded to give me instructions. "Take the bus to Bakersfield, then to Barstow, then catch a bus north. You may have to hitchhike the last few miles." Another pause. "You're to go to Sunset Estates and ask for Mrs. Peabody, she'll find you a place to crash. We'll be down there later in the week, so just wait for us. And Gusti—"

"Yes?"

"Take care of your ankle."

I said I would. I wanted to add my sincere appreciation for all the help she had given me but at that moment the operator cut in demanding more change, which I didn't have, so that had to be all of it.

MR. FAWCETT'S EMPIRE

Sunset Estates turned out a lot grander than I had anticipated. There were perhaps sixty townhouse units, some for rent, all for sale, agreeably placed among the pines and boulders; an artificial lake had been scooped out and a community clubhouse built on its shores. There were four tennis courts, a sports boutique, an exercise room, sauna, whirlpool and a waterfall and cold plunge in a rock grotto. There were also billiards, table-tennis and, for the sedentary, gaming tables carved out of pine burls. There was an electronic game room for the children, two lounge-bars, a franchised restaurant and a corral with three sad-faced donkeys and a cowboy-guide. Someone had put a lot of money into the project, although as yet there were distressingly few owners in residence.

At Reception I asked for Mrs. Peabody. To my surprise the owner of that most Anglo of names turned out to be Chinese. But Chinese with a difference—she looked like one of those Asian movie stars you see on the posters: a perfect round face, like a peach, only with just a bit too much rouge on its cheeks. She spoke flawless BBC-style English and carried a heavily-scented pigskin attaché-case—the perfect New Wave executive. All the lighting fixtures in her office were made of folded *origami* papers, and there was a poster over her desk with a lot of Chinese writing and a drawing of a giant rodent with boxing gloves and a menacing posture. In English it said: IT'S THE YEAR OF THE RAT— DON'T GIVE UP THE SHIP. I hadn't the slightest idea what the rat was doing there. But then I wasn't too sure what *I* was up to, either.

Mrs. Peabody was cordial. Yes, she had been expecting me. Yes, Mr. Fawcett had called just that morning. Indeed, she would be delighted to show me the courts and clubhouse. But first she would take me to my apartment. We paused to inspect the glassed-in scale model of Sunset Estates, both present and projected (another eighty units were in the planning stages, she informed me) and I was introduced to the two salesmen (the closers, Mr. Fawcett had called them). I didn't get their full names but that didn't matter as all the time I was at Dinosaur nobody called them anything but "Benson" and "Kokomo". Right now, for lack of customers, they were playing pinochle in their office. Benson looked like a border-town Texas sheriff; Kokomo was Korean and wore heavily-tinted sports goggles and a permanent toothpaste smile. A pair of bandits, I thought—an opinion I wasn't to change.

Compared to anything I had previously encountered on my tour, my apartment was luxurious. I think its only disadvantage was the granite cliff up against the picture window, which must have made it hard to sell. Otherwise, it had everything—air conditioning, garbage dispose-all and heated towel racks in the spacious Italian tile bathroom. I began to feel like a millionaire.

For the next three days I did nothing much but rest and enjoy the pine-scented air which reminded me of boyhood trips on the slopes of Mt. Popo. I explored the village, took the gondola to the top of the mountain, and charged some new tennis clothes at the resort's *boutique*. For now my duties were simple: to put out the nets in the morning, make myself visible on the courts when customers came calling, give an occasional duffer lesson, and to take down the nets at dusk. A piece of cake.

Then on Friday Vicki showed up with Mr. Fawcett.

Her big news was that she had gotten a letter from Sabrina, with another enclosed for me:

Dearest Agosto—

We were back in Auckland for supplies and fresh drinking water and so forth so at *last* I've a little time to write. What a *challenge* the last six weeks have been! It's really and truly—no bullshit—as if my life has been stood on its head. I've been working day and night as "messperson" for a crew of fourteen—that includes the photographer and the medical doctor—assembled from all over the world—even two Yugoslavs and an Algerian! Since I'm about the messiest person in the State of Washington, *mess-person* is the right title for me. What it means is swabbing down the galley, washing dishes and serving meals for *everybody* plus "prepping" the veggies for cook.

We've been half-way to Antarctica and back by way of Tahiti, Bora-Bora and *Les Isles sous le Vent*. What a trip! And the *Mercurio*—that's us—doesn't have a stabilizer so I've been sick a lot, what with rolling and pitching and a big storm we hit off South Island. The pitching fore-and-aft is worse. Yuk! You wouldn't recognize me, I'm so thin. There's nothing like sea-sickness to bring out your latent anorexia.

Vicki says you've met Mother and Hizzoner the Papal Monster. So what else is new? My spies on Bainbridge report that Father and Cappy have had a simply *dreadful* fight—though what about nobody seems to know—genealogy I should imagine—and that Cappy has left and gone back to teaching 18th century literature in an obscure little college in Minnesota or Saskatchewan or some equally flattened-out place. Poor Cappy! He has a wonderful mind and it deserves better than to live in that utterly *flaccid* body, doesn't it? Father of course is just being his usual hypocritical defensive self for which I don't much blame him—he can't cope with emotion. He's always been that way.

God! I hope it isn't hereditary!

Here, the sun shines every single day—even tho it rains *almost* every afternoon—and we've put the spotlight of publicity on three different illegal whalers, catching them right in the midst of the most *dreadful* butchery of our fellow mammals. Peter and Nigel—they're our leaders—say we're at the cutting edge of the international conscience (how's that for a mixed metaphor?) tho there *are* days—fortunately this isn't one of them—when I feel that if anyone is at the edge of being cut up it must be me.

Dear Agosto,

I think of you a lot though you wouldn't guess it from my long silence. I *know* we are going to meet again though we may be changed so much we won't recognize each other. Or like what we see. But we *will* meet. Where??? How about half way—Machu Pichu? Or Trinidad? Or next Xmas in Rio de Janeiro? I've pretty much had it with Seattle and there's no reason to stay in Dullsville, U.S.A. when I've got the money to travel, is there?

But first I've got a stack of dirty dishes a yard high to wash and the cook is yelling for me—the poor baby needs his potatoes peeled. So dreams and all that loftier shit will have to wait—

Do write—Vicki knows where—

        A big greasy kiss—
        S—

I showed the letter to Vicki and asked her opinion. "Vintage Sabrina," she said drily. It was obvious she was no longer as enchanted by Sabrina as she once had been. Or perhaps it was only the strain of a very difficult drive down. Mr. Fawcett had hitched a trailer onto the Bentley and had driven from Berkeley over the Tioga Pass with a tank full of *koi*, a kind of Oriental golden carp, stopping every twenty miles to make sure none of them had spilled out or were suffering unduly from travel sickness. "Wilder is just impossible about those fucking fish," Vicki said. "He's a monomaniac. Unfortunately, you never know from one day to the next what his mania is going to be." Of course the fish were immediately transferred—wriggling and well—to the artificial pond, but that wasn't the end of it. The next morning when I went out to hang up the nets on the tennis courts, there was my employer, sloshing around in the mud in hip-boots. He was, he said, planting water lilies.

"These *koi*," he told me, "will adapt to almost any environment. It helps, though, if they think they are in Japan. The pH factor in the water," he added, "is also important."

"They'll be beautiful," I said.

"The fish? The fish are hiding now."

"I meant the water lilies. I like them. They're—well, they're serene."

Mr. Fawcett transferred his attention from the plants to me; this remark seemed to interest him.

"You like bareback riders and now water lilies. I think you have a streak of the poet in you, young man."

I didn't deny it. After all, didn't Guillermo Vilas, who had been my boyhood idol, write poetry? Mr. Fawcett then shifted the conversation.

"Has the dragon-lady looked after you?"

"Mrs. Peabody?"

"Yes."

"She has been very kind."

"Good." Mr. Fawcett, the last of the water lilies suitably anchored, began cleaning off his spade. "She's the watchdog here, you know."

I said that she seemed very efficient.

"She is that," he said a bit grimly. "But she's not *my* watchdog. Or perhaps she is. By which I mean, she's hired to watch *me*. Help me off with these boots, will you? They stick."

"Really?" I said, tugging at one muddy boot. "I thought she was your assistant."

"No way," said Mr. Fawcett. "She belongs to my partners. Or maybe they belong to her. Some day you'll meet them strolling about. Hong Kong. Baskets of money but not much savvy as to what Dick and Jane want. Or will buy. But they call the shots, and dragon-lady is their enforcer. She has to approve everything, even the water lilies."

"And does she like them?"

"Oh, she likes them well enough. But she's worried about maintenance. It freezes here in the winter, you know."

"It freezes in Japan, too."

"Yes, but not in Hong Kong."

Mr. Fawcett stretched out on the bank and surveyed his work with satisfaction mingled with a certain sadness; perhaps he was thinking of the frosty days soon to come.

"You know," he said at last. "Some day I'm going to chuck all this."

"What will you do then?"

"Sit under a willow tree and meditate. Perhaps write a book. Of reflections and proverbs. Like Marcus Aurelius. You know Marcus Aurelius?"

"Certainly," I said. "Marcus Aurelius was the thirteenth Roman emperor."

"You continually amaze me, young man. How on earth did you know that?"

"Because I am named after the first Roman emperor, Caesar Augustus. Naturally, when I was in school I learned who my heirs were. Augustus, Tiberius, Caligula, Claudius, Nero—" I began rattling them off.

"I believe you, I believe you," Mr. Fawcett interrupted. "But the important thing about Marcus Aurelius was that when he grew tired of his empire he began to write philosophy. That's what we have in common—or would have, if I could ever get the time. Now, shall we have a set of tennis? Just to give you a warm-up—I'm completely out of shape."

He may have been out of shape but he played a remarkably good game for an amateur—dashing and venturesome, although lacking the patience to hold the back-court and an easy victim to my passing shots. But as in everything he did, his energy and enthusiasm carried him buoyantly along. Mr. Fawcett had *verve*, he always seemed to be playing over his head.

No Bingo, No Obligation

The meeting was dragging to a close.

"And now for today's philosophical morsel," Mr. Fawcett said, trying to balance his coffee saucer on edge with the help of a soggy paper napkin. "It may interest you all to know that in the Battle of Crécy in 1346 there were perhaps 25,000 men involved on *both* sides, four or five thousand of whom ended up dead on the battlefield. Last year alone in the United States of America more than 20,000 persons were murdered. Twenty thousand—pffft!" He cut his own throat with an extended forefinger.

"In cold blood or hot blood?" asked the ever-practical Vicki.

"The statistics don't say," answered Mr. Fawcett, giving up on the saucer. "My point is that on the streets of the American city and over the gleaming linoleum of the American bathroom carnage is being wrought that dwarfs all the battles of classical history."

"Wilder is full of these discoveries," Vicki explained to me in a whisper.

"I don't understand the significance of these data," said Mrs. Peabody in her clipped British. "As recently as twenty years ago perhaps five hundred thousand human beings were slaughtered in one week in Indonesia. At least one hundred thousand were ethnic Chinese. No one in the civilized world seemed greatly disturbed." There was no mistaking the knife-edge of irony in her "civilized".

"One hundred and forty thousand were killed in one instant at Hiroshima," I put in.

"Progress, you see, progress. Which reminds me," Mr. Fawcett went on. "Hong Kong has been on the phone again. They say they're out of French Provincial cookware. They can let us have all-electric *woks* instead."

The salesmen were quick to protest this change in giveaways.

"The casseroles are our most popular item," Benson said. Kokomo backed him up: "*Woks* will have zero appeal. Even the Asians are switching out of them."

Mr. Fawcett disagreed. "They're popular with the Yuppie crowd and they're the ones we've got to target. Anyway, we can still offer the Orlon aviation luggage to clients who don't want *woks*."

"The handles are falling off," Benson said glumly. "I get one complaint I get a dozen—crappy seams and no stability in the handles."

"There is a form you can file," Mrs. Peabody said frostily. "If the gifts are faulty we will make restitution. But only with the proper form."

"And Yuppies!" Benson exploded, his jowls shaking and his broad sheriff's face redder than usual. "Who needs them? They got one eye on the door all the time you're pitching them. They take your Taiwan airplane luggage and they grab the next flight to Hawaii or Cancun. Not only does the luggage fall apart but it puts the wrong idea in their heads. What we want is that plumber and his mousy little wife from North Platte, the ones I sold #37 to last week. Free cookware! You should have seen her eyes light up. Cookware, you don't have to risk your life flying, and Bingo games—that's what brings 'em in. Never mind the Yuppies."

"Our plans," said Mrs. Peabody, cool in the face of this onslaught, "are to move Sunset Estates gradually upscale. We envisage a world-class destination."

"Which your plumber and his wife can share," Mr. Fawcett added, to mollify his salesman.

"But no Bingo?"

"I think at present definitely no Bingo."

Mrs. Peabody nodded her agreement.

There was a dead silence in which the advocates of two differing visions of the good life glared at one another. It was Vicki who broke the tension.

"More coffee, anyone?"

"And that's another thing—" We all knew Benson was about to start in again on the quality, or lack of it, of the coffee; nobody wanted to listen to him since it had long been apparent that nothing would ever be done about it.

"I guess that about wraps it up," Mr. Fawcett said, springing to his feet. "Energy and optimism, gang, that's the secret!"

And another day's sales conference was over.

Vicki and I put in two or three hours every day in the village distributing brochures and talking up tours of the resort with energy and optimism. We worked the restaurants and particularly the exit door from the gondolas which went up Dinosaur Mountain. People coming out that door were likely to be either exhilarated or exhausted—in either case their defenses were down.

"Concentrate on couples," Vicki advised me. "The boys don't like to work singles; they get a client sold and then they have to start all over again with the spouse. So always go for two at once." I was also instructed to keep my eye open for Hispanic couples, largely day-trippers from Los Angeles, although I was to discover that most of them had mixed feelings about the romance of mountain living. I think Mexicans in particular have been brought up to view rocky peaks and thin air as something to be avoided; in any event, despite my optimism and perfect Spanish, we made no sales in that direction during my stay at Dinosaur.

Vicki did a lot better. She had a clear, forthright and neighborly approach that inspired confidence. "And I don't try to sell anything," she explained. "The first pitch is just to get acquainted. You've got to show an interest in the clients—where they come from and how their kids are doing in school. Leave the hard sell to the closers, that's their specialty. We're just out to make friends. No obligation and free cookware. Stick with it, Gusti, you'll get the hang of it after a few days."

But of course I never did. Perhaps I am too passive ever to be a successful salesman. And I could never quite avoid putting myself in the victim's shoes and thinking of all the reasons why he *shouldn't* part with his hard-won money for a lifetime exposure to alpine boredom. Plainly, I didn't inspire boundless confidence.

There was another reason, too, for our generally sluggish sales.

"This spread is strictly for ski bunnies," Benson informed me after a particularly disheartening day. "It needs snow to make it go." Most time-slots from Thanksgiving to April had already been sold, leaving the rest of the year—which nobody rushed to purchase. "Without the white stuff, what's here? No fishee, no huntee, no nookie. That leaves us with clean, wholesome donkey rides, peewee golf and a restaurant that don't know how to make a decent cup of coffee. You take it, buddy. Come Labor Day I'm moving on to Vegas. I can make more bucks than this dealing stud." Kokomo was equally pessimistic but planned to stay on till the winter influx livened things up. "It's that or go back to Brandeis and learn computers," he said. Neither option seemed to appeal to him. Meanwhile, some of the condos were on short-term rental but most stood vacant while Fawcett, Peabody and the distant partners ran up vast trans-Pacific phone bills trying to figure out, on alternate days, how to draw the public in or how to cut the overhead.

An active, advertised tennis program had been one such ploy, but even the chance to study with a world-class Uruguayan star didn't have many takers. I dealt with a succession of unwilling children parked by their parents for an hour or two under my supervision and a few members of a Japanese tour who wanted to get some exercise after long hours in a chartered bus. None of them showed much promise. Then, in my third week at Sunset Estates, I acquired a student who was to change all that.

Unexpected Drop Shots

I was in a bad mood. Mrs. Peabody had just called me into her office to complain about the bills I was running up at the boutique. I had countered by pointing out that in two weeks I had received no pay at all for my services. She then referred to my immigration status. "Naturally," she said, "the company can't authorize illegal checks. I understood that all payments were to be deferred until Mr. Fawcett has cleared your status." When would that be? No one seemed certain. "It is being processed," she said coolly. To which I answered that I was sure Sunset Estates expected me to dress properly for my role as resident professional. Grudgingly, she agreed, and we left it at that. But all the same I had a familiar sinking feeling; my travels had taught me that America did not always fulfill its glowing promises.

So I was a bit short with my new student, who had paid in advance for an hour's instruction. He seemed an unlikely prospect—slight, slender and pallid, he was dressed in too-neatly-pressed white shorts and shirt; on his forehead he wore a green plastic eyeshield more appropriate to a bookkeeper than a tennis player. Yet he was earnest and appeared eager to learn. And on the court he turned out to be surprisingly agile. He had a fine assortment of chips, lobs, chops and drop shots, the equipment of what is generally called a clay court player. In fact, he was about as good as he possibly could be with no athleticism. He simply had no strength or stamina, but all that deftness and cunning could provide he had, plus an ability to cover the court and get seemingly impossible shots back. We rallied for perhaps fifteen minutes and then I gave him some instruction in volleying and covering the net, areas of obvious weakness in his game.

"Now," he said at last, "I'm out of breath. It's the smoke in the air." He waved toward the hazy sky; there were brush fires a few kilometers away which had overcast Dinosaur Mountain. "Could we rest a bit? I want to talk to you about something else."

We went into the clubroom. There was no one around but the girl who tended the boutique. My student bought sodas from the machine. I noticed now that he had brown, spaniel eyes and a perpetually worried way of biting his lip. I offered him a chair but he declined. "I think best on my feet." So he paced around the billiard table, occasionally leaning on it as if it were a podium.

"I am an attorney," he said apologetically, almost as if he expected me to spring away in revulsion. "I only play tennis on weekends."

"I didn't think you played all the time," I said with a friendly laugh.

"You don't understand. My name is Fogarty, Philip S. Fogarty. You have heard of me?"

Indeed I had, although I wasn't about to admit it. In a state of shock I mumbled, "I don't really believe so."

"I called on you. At your hotel in San Francisco. You were out, I believe. At that point in time."

"Fogarty?"

"Yes, Fogarty."

I put down my Gatorade as if a great shaft of light had just opened my skull. "Oh, *that* Mr. Fogarty! Of course, of course. I meant to return your call, Mr. Fogarty, I had every intention, but the sudden sickness of my brother's little boy interfered. I had to rush over and take him out of school. Scarlet fever is so contagious, you know."

"I hope he's feeling better now," Mr. Fogarty said sympathetically.

"Completely recovered. Just a scar or two. He's back with his mother now . . . in Guadalajara."

The claims of compassion satisfied, Mr. Fogarty returned to his subject. "As you may know, César, I represent a number of the investors in Plains of Plenty."

"Plains of Plenty?"

"The cattle resettling venture with which I believe you are, at this point in time, associated."

"I wouldn't call it associated, sir."

"No? And what would you call it? You are listed on its board of directors."

"True," I said pleasantly, "but I am only a *prestanombre*."

Mr. Fogarty said that he was unfamiliar with that term.

"It's Spanish for someone who lends his name to a business."

"Yes, yes, a fine word—that's just what I thought—a *prestanombre*—an excellent word."

"They needed another Uruguayan on the incorporation papers."

"I see, I see!" he said, apparently greatly cheered. "It's just what I thought—you are every bit as much a victim of these people as my clients were!"

I agreed that this might be the case.

"I knew it, César, I knew it. That's what I thought all along." Then he paused, leaned toward me across the billiard table and bit his lower lip. "My difficulty—and it has been a substantial difficulty, César—has been in convincing my clients of that. Some of them have been—how shall I put it?—yes, *blinded* by the magnitude of their losses and—quite irrationally, I am sure—tend to strike out in all directions, causing the innocent to suffer along with the guilty. That is the real tragedy of this affair."

I said that in my opinion the real tragedy was the murder of Mr. William P. Wetherall.

"Please, César, please!" Mr. Fogarty implored. "You mustn't for a single moment think that my clients were in any way, shape or manner, either directly or tangentially involved in that lamentable event. My clients are men of substance in the community, physicians, agriculturists, reputable investors. They were every bit as horrified as you and I by the circumstances surrounding Mr. Wetherall's departure. You must believe that, César."

I didn't believe a word of it, but said, as pleasantly as I could, that such a thought had never crossed my mind.

"Mr. Wetherall was in the shrimp business," he went on, "and there are a lot of Colombians and Vietnamese involved in that trade, people who don't have our concept of the value of human life. No doubt one of them chose to settle accounts with him."

"No doubt."

"But there is going to be litigation arising out of this case," he said with barely concealed satisfaction at the prospect. "Substantial amounts of litigation. I make no secret of that fact. The investors in Plains of Plenty are going to recover what they can from the estate of the late Mr. Wetherall, which still has substantial assets, particularly in seafood. And my over-riding concern, César, is to protect you from the consequences of any such litigation. There may well be criminal prosecution for securities fraud as well."

He paused, both hands pressed downward on the billiard table, seeming to await my decision on this crucial issue. I asked him what I should do.

"I can't represent you, César," he said regretfully, "since legally we are, at this point in time, in an adversarial posture. But, speaking strictly as your friend and tennis student, my advice is to seek counsel. Seek counsel, César, and without undue delay file an affidavit—which I should be happy to bring to the attention of my clients—stating the true facts of your involvement in this case and establishing, without fear of contradiction, that you too were an unwitting victim of these swindlers. With such an affidavit duly signed and attested, it might be possible for you to join in the action against the Wetherall estate and recover your own personal losses. But time is of the essence, César, you must strike while the iron is hot. He who hesitates is, as Shakespeare says, irrevocably lost."

With this eloquent peroration he concluded his presentation. We drank the rest of our Gatorades in silence and went back to the tennis court. Naturally, my concentration had been destroyed and I played very badly. Disaster seemed to be closing in all around me.

When the hour was finally up Mr. Fogarty thanked me effusively. "You've given me some wonderful pointers," he said, shaking my hand. "I hope we get a chance to work together again soon." He pointed out that he and his wife were staying at the nearby Wildwood Inn and suggested that we get together for a drink. "She'd love to meet you, César. We're combining a little business with a vacation, you know." I made my excuses. "Tell you what," he suggested brightly. "Suppose I drop by in the morning? There's a notary public in the village who'll be in her office by ten, and I could help you draft up an affidavit, if you decide to go that way."

All right? Look for me around nine-thirty."

"I will, sir."

"Phil. It's just Phil. I can't stand all that formality."

"Okay . . . Phil."

"See ya." And he was gone.

What was I to do? It was perfectly clear that what he wanted out of me was an affidavit that would help convict Albert and Mr. Wetherall, *in absentia*, of fraud. It was also plain that he was prepared to use persuasion, wiles and threats, perhaps even violence, to get it. I thought of Mr. Wetherall's body stuffed in the trunk of that limousine and shivered. Was that my future, too? Not that I really cared too much about Mr. Wetherall's posthumous reputation—he was one American I had never much liked; but to betray Phyllis and Albert, my friends and patrons, in exchange for my own temporary safety seemed the way of a coward and ingrate. And then there were the Uruguayans to consider. The man whom I have called Mr. Z—was a powerful politician close to the president. I shuddered to think what might happen to me in Montevideo if the Americans tried to extradite him for fraud, based even so slightly on my sworn testimony. No, it was a dreadful mess whichever way I went.

Utterly depressed and more than a little confused, I decided to ask Vicki for advice. It was a lucky move.

ON THE ROAD AGAIN

"Poor Gusti!" Vicki said. "You certainly have a talent for jumping out of the kettle into the fire." She had listened carefully to the account of my involvement in the affairs of Mr. Wetherall and his Plains of Plenty. I held nothing back. Only one thing puzzled her.

"How in God's name did they track you down here?"

"I have no idea." And I hadn't. It seemed an almost supernatural piece of sleuthing.

"Unless they were shadowing the Bentley, too," Vicki ventured.

"Yes, they could be after you and Wilder."

"Come off it," Vicki said and punched me, a sisterly blow. "One thing is obvious, Gusti—"

"Not to me."

"Well, it should be. No affidavit. You don't sign anything."

"I thought you'd say that."

"Of course I say it. It's only common sense. If there's an indictment they'll hold you as a material witness. Even if there isn't, your name will go on the police computer and you'll have everybody after you, including the Seattle D.A."

"Christ!" I said. "I'd forgotten Dr. Kains."

"Well, they haven't."

"But what do I do?"

"Split. Skip the country. *Muy pronto.* Head for your sister's wedding. Make one of the party. Blend in." She was now launched on her favorite role—the executive. "I'll drive you to Barstow first thing in the morning. We won't take the Bentley—that's too conspicuous in case they're putting a tail on you. Catch the Las Vegas to L.A. bus, take another to San Diego and the trolley to the border. Walk across. The Mexicans won't give you any trouble, will they?"

"No, I have dual citizenship."

"Well, there you are. Out of sight in Ensenada. And Mr. Foggerty can go whistle for his affidavit."

"I'll do it," I said resolutely and gave her a big hug with my thanks. She returned me a wry smile and said, "That's what old friends are for."

We found Mr. Fawcett out by the entrance to Sunset Estates with two stonemasons. He took the news of my departure calmly enough. "This is going to be absolutely smashing," he said with his old enthusiasm. "Think of it! An eighteen foot natural waterfall right where you drive in. And lit up every night by waterproof lighting right inside the fall! It's going to be the show piece on the whole mountain."

"I'm taking the lodge van down to Barstow," Vicki informed him.

"You do that. Sorry to lose you, young man. But when you get back I'll have a work permit for you. Tennis is going to be in our future. In a big way."

There was no mention of the rather scanty commissions I had earned for steering customers to the Closers, but later that afternoon Mr. Fawcett took me into the boutique where he and Vicki selected a very expensive light brown alpaca jacket and a couple of pairs of slacks for me.

"You can't go to a wedding in tennis whites," he observed. "If you're going to represent the firm you'll have to look the part."

"He looks very handsome," Vicki observed in an objective tone.

"Of course he does, Victoria. He's *our* champion."
I thanked them both very sincerely, but couldn't resist remarking that Mrs. Peabody was sure to be upset by the expense.

"Fuck Mrs. Peabody," Mr. Fawcett said loftily. And then added, "Only metaphorically, of course."

At daybreak next morning we started the long drive south. Coming down the winding road from Dinosaur to the Owens Valley we were followed by a very official-looking Chevrolet sedan. "It's someone going to work early in Bishop," Vicki said. "Maybe the geologists or forest service people." All the same, I was nervous; someone had tracked me to this out-of-the-way spot and I didn't expect them to let me escape their clutches so easily. For half an hour they followed us closely and only when the highway finally straight-ened out did they speed up and pass. Vicki was right. The car carried two men in hard hats and bore the markings of the Bureau of Land Management.

"How did you know?" I asked her.

"Simple. They had federal license plates, and the Immies don't work this far north." Vicki had sharp eyes.

We passed through Bishop just as the sun was coming up over the White Mountains in Nevada. The town was still asleep.

"There's nobody behind us," Vicki assured me. "Relax. Unless your friend Foggerty can rent a helicopter you're home free."

The scenery was spectacular. To our right, illuminated by the first rays of sunlight was the great escarpment of the Sierra Nevada; even this late in the year there were patches of snow and ice gleaming in the new light. Somewhere ahead, among that jumble of crags, was Mount Whitney, the loftiest peak in the

U.S.A., but I couldn't tell where. The haze from the brush fires had cleared away and the mountains seemed startlingly close above us. Closer at hand, the valley was dotted with range cattle, beginning their morning's preoccupation with grass. What a vast and strange country this is, I thought, but, since that was an obvious cliché felt by every traveller in North America, I kept it to myself.

Nor was Vicki very communicative. From time to time she gave me a sideways glance, as if to make sure I was still there, but otherwise her thoughts seemed to be a long way off. It was only when we had passed Lone Pine and begun the descent into the blazing heat of the desert that she opened up a bit.

"I'm not a morning person," she said. "I was brought up in the desert, you know, and I'm like the lizards—I don't wake up until I feel the heat."

"I didn't know. I thought you were from Seattle."

She laughed. "Not me. Seattle was just another by-product of a lousy marriage. I'm a Southern Californian. Palm Springs. Or anyway, that's what I tell people. Actually, it was Indio—the other side of the tracks."

"The tracks?" The expression puzzled me.

"It means I'm just a poor working girl who likes to pretend."

"To pretend what?"

"God, you're inquisitive! To pretend that she was brought up among the rich and famous. That's what Palm Springs means, isn't it?"

I said I really wasn't familiar with Palm Springs.

"Lucky you. It's full of millionaires and similar assholes. And it's an utter, total hell if you're an adolescent with two pairs of jeans and one homemade orlon dress. And you ride to school on a broken-down

bicycle with a loose chain while everybody else gets there in their Porsches and Jaguars. That's Palm Springs."
After this outburst she fell silent again. But for the first time I began to understand Vicki and empathize with her; poverty and what it meant to a child were certainly no strangers to me.

It was nearly eleven when we got to Barstow, an ugly little town in the midst of the sagebrush. We stopped for breakfast and there Vicki came up with a new plan. Perhaps she had been thinking it up during her long silences.

"You're going to get hopelessly lost in L.A., Gusti," she said over coffee.

"No, I won't. I could find my way around Tokyo—Los Angeles doesn't scare me."

"You don't know what a snakepit it is. No, I think I'd better drive you to the border myself."

"It's a long way."

"Not all that far. We can avoid L.A. completely and take the desert route to Mexicali. I can make it in five hours. And tomorrow you can grab a Mexican bus to Tijuana and save all sorts of money. They cost hardly anything."

The idea was certainly attractive, but I said I didn't think I ought to put her to all that driving—she had already taken me over 300 kilometers.

"No big deal," she said. "I like driving. Particularly through the desert. Besides, I want to stop in Indio and see Nana."

"Nana?"

"My grandmother. My Armenian grandmother. She still lives there. I think she misses me."

So instead of saying goodbye in Barstow we got back into the van and headed toward Victorville and the Mojave Desert. Of course, the moment she suggested it I knew that she couldn't get back to Dinosaur that night, so I asked her what Mr. Fawcett would say.

"Wilder," she said, "can go take a flying leap at the moon for all I care." This attitude was decidedly new and it got my attention. "Mr. Wilder Fawcett may be a genius, but he is also a total sleaze. At this precise moment I'm sure he's trying to put the make on one of those darling little cocktail sluts at the Timbertop Club."

This had the unmistakable accent of the Wronged Woman, so I shifted ground and asked about her family. I'd always thought her a Northwest Anglo, so the Armenian grandmother out in the Mojave came as quite a shock.

"My father was an immigrant from Erevan," Vicki said. "He worked on the citrus ranches around Coachella. I don't remember him very well; I was only six when he was killed—in a tractor accident. It hit soft dirt on the edge of an irrigation ditch and rolled over on him. He was bleeding internally. And I guess it took him a long time to die—that's what my mother said, anyway. Of course, I don't remember much of it." Her mother had married again, to a petty officer in the Navy, and had moved away to San Diego, leaving her daughter with her father's family who had all followed him to America. Vicki said she didn't see her mother often. "She drinks." She said that as you might say *She's a Roman Catholic* or *She's a seamstress*. It wasn't an accusation, simply a nametag.

But from here on things began to change. It was as if Vicki and I had reached an unspoken understanding. What that understanding was I am still not sure; perhaps it was the recognition that we had travelled the same lonely landscape and could recognize all the rivers and buttes and milestones along the way. Or perhaps it was nothing so profound, merely shared mutual hungers. Up to a day or so ago I had thought of her mainly as my employer's mistress and Sabrina's best friend; then it had dawned on me that she didn't really like Sabrina and that she and Mr. Fawcett were following utterly divergent paths. Whatever it was, from this time on Vicki and I looked at one another with different eyes; it was as if some new continent had suddenly come up over the horizon, presenting us both with the challenges and distresses that only explorers can know.

Homecomings

As we approached Indio I saw acres of stately date palms, which gave the desert a welcome gray-green plumage. The town itself was depressing. There were railroad tracks, a lot of dusty pickups, and the traffic signs were full of bullet holes. On the outskirts Vicki slowed the van at a palm grove. "This is it," she said. We drew up beside a ramshackle shed where a sign said L. TRAVAKIAN - DATES - NUTS - DRIED FRUIT. Larger hand-painted signs advertised seasonal specials in melons. An overweight spotted dog lay panting in the meagre midday shade. It was blistering hot and no one else was visible. But there was a bell on the sales counter and Vicki rang it vigorously.

"Everyone's asleep," she said. "Things haven't changed a bit."

But they weren't. At the sound of the bell two women emerged from opposite ends of the shed. Apparently they were Vicki's aunt and cousin, for when they saw her they burst into effusions of Armenian. I was duly introduced in a few words of English, but they quickly reverted to their native tongue, probably, I thought, because they didn't want me to hear what they had to say to Vicki. The aunt had a crooked mouth and peroxided hair set in pink plastic curlers. She had an unpleasantly loud voice and seemed to be alternately welcoming and reproaching her wayward niece.

Vicki explained that her uncle Levon and his son-in-law were aloft in a date-palm cleaning out rats' nests but that another cousin had been sent for him. Meanwhile, we all went into the old frame house behind the store to visit Vicki's grandmother who was a wizened old woman dressed in total black and asleep in a tattered overstuffed chair. She looked just like an old *campesina* you might run across in some forgotten village in Guerrero or Michoacán. On the table beside her there was a noisy electric fan which kept blowing wisps of gray hair across her wrinkled face. "Wake up, mama, you're catching flies," the aunt said in English. The old lady snapped awake and she, too, fell to shouting Armenian at her granddaughter. It was a very confused scene.

While we waited for the men in the family we were treated to a cold fruit soup, hard bread and slices of iced Persian melon. In that dreadful heat nothing could have been more welcome. Then a messenger arrived from the date orchard announcing a delay; a workman had borrowed the extension ladder and Uncle Levon was temporarily trapped forty feet off the ground. Vicki, who had by now thoroughly hugged and shed tears of joy over her grandmother, seized this opportunity to get away. Laden with bags of dates and accompanied by loud farewells which, to my ears, sounded strangely like curses, we drove off southward toward Mexico.

"What was your aunt telling you?" I asked after we had had time to calm down.

Vicki didn't answer right away.

"She was furious with me for not staying longer. And she said I was a fool for travelling around with a nineteen-year-old boy."

"I'm twenty-two," I protested.

"I know. But that's what she said. She likes to exaggerate."

"And what did you say?"

"I told her what I've always told her—that she should

learn to keep her nose out of other people's business. And that you weren't just a pretty-boy—that's what she called you."

"And your grandmother?"

"Nana?"

"Yes. What did she call me?"

"I don't think she even noticed you, Gusti. She's very nearly blind. Nana was angry with me because I hadn't been to see her."

"But you *were* there."

"I know. But with Nana the present doesn't count for much. It's what you have or haven't done in the past that's really important."

"Your cousin yelled at you, too."

"My cousins all hate me," Vicki said with a laugh. "They're pissed because I had the nerve to get out of Indio, while they're still stuck there."

I sighed.

"It was all very Mexican," I said.

"You thought so?"

"Yes. I felt right at home. If only I could have spoken Armenian."

She gave my knee a squeeze. "You're a dear, Gusti." And then switched the subject. "We're going to pass the Salton Sea in a minute."

"I don't know it. Is it a real sea?"

"No, it's a mistake. Some land developers caused it. They were trying to divert the Colorado River and something went wrong with their arithmetic."

After a while we did indeed come to the Salton Sea.

"It isn't much," Vicki said.

I agreed with her. It was a sort of 40 kilometer long catch-basin with flat unvegetated shores.

"It would be better," Vicki said. "If the shores were more reliable. But the water rises for a few years and then it sinks again. No one knows for sure where it's going to be from one season to the next. It makes it impossible to build anything worthwhile."

"Too bad," I said and thought of flower-bright Lake Xochimilco which virtually had dried up and been covered by Mexico City's slums.

"Right now I think it's shrinking." She drove faster. The road kept a safe distance from the unpredictable Salton. "I think you would have liked my Uncle Levon. He tells wonderful stories. I'm sorry he couldn't get down from the tree; he likes talking to people in English."

"Perhaps when I come back I can visit him."

"Perhaps. Perhaps then." But I knew she didn't believe me.

At El Centro there were signs all along the highway advertising Mexican auto insurance. "Your U. S. policy is no good on the other side," I warned her.

"I know, I know," she answered. "But I'm not staying long enough to make it worth while." Just the same, she stopped at one of the stores and re-emerged a few minutes later with a pack of condoms.

"That's all the insurance I'll be needing." She tossed me the pack. "You know the Girl Scout motto."

"No. I've never met any Girl Scouts. What is it?"

"Don't leave home without it."

We both laughed. I was definitely getting physically interested in Vicki.

At the border there was heavy rush-hour traffic between Calexico and Mexicali and we had to wait in line. While we were held up an American official approached the car. I had a shiver of apprehension—was I going to be arrested only fifty meters from safety? The official stared fixedly at me as if to read my most secret and illegal thoughts. But he was only conducting a survey for the Imperial County Water Commission. Did we own or rent? If the former, how often did we turn on our lawn sprinklers? Had we installed water-saving devices in our toilets? And so forth. Vicki gave him detailed if fictitious answers while I tried to keep a straight face. Then we crossed into Mexico which was no problem at all—the difficulties all lie in travelling the other direction. Vicki drove carefully through the noisy, confusing town center and proceeded down a four-lane parkway with blighted palm trees in the divider until we came to signs for *El Conquistador Motel-Color TV-Pool-Sauna.*

"El Conquistador," she said. "Why don't they ever have a motel La Conquistadora?"

"Because Cortéz didn't have any women soldiers in his army."

"You think that's the reason?"

"Sure. What else?"

She studied me a moment before answering.

"I think you've got some things to learn, Gusti."

"I'm always a willing student," I said and put my hand on her thigh.

After a minute or so we got out of the car. It was hot as the inside of a kiln. I went in and registered for us both. The rates were in dollars; pesos didn't seem to be in much demand. When we opened the door to our room we were hit by a frosty blast of Made-in-the-USA air-conditioning. I began to sneeze.

"That won't do," Vicki said, pulling the drapes shut. "Get into bed, Gusti. I'm going to turn the air-conditioning off." And after a moment's reflection she added, "We're going to work up a sweat and I wouldn't want you to catch cold your first day in Mexico."

Next morning Vicki drove me to the bus station. I kissed her good-bye, tenderly, and remarked on the irony of having to part just when we were commencing to know one another.

"There is a Spanish proverb that goes—." But Vicki cut me off.

"No old Spanish proverbs today, Gusti. Please. I don't think I could take one right now." But she saw my concern and acknowledged it. "Don't worry about me— I've done graduate work in good-byes." And kissed me once more and was gone.

Right here, in Mexico at last and relatively safe from pursuit, my story ought to end. My voyages in North America were over. Of course, next year when things had quieted down I might return. I had promised Nikki Fassmyer to be back in Oregon to defend our title, and now I had made implicit pledges to both Vicki and Mr. Fawcett as well, but if I did return it would no longer be as the naïve tourist who had taken the ferry from British Columbia three months before. No, any return would be with new, with different eyes; I would be a wiser, a tougher César-Agosto, perhaps one more worthy of that imperial name. As the Americans liked to say, now *I knew the ropes*.

So I am tempted to call it quits right here in the Mexicali station of the *Tres Estrellas de Oro* bus line. But then, if you have stuck with my story this far, you are certainly entitled to know how certain events turned out, in particular my sister Celestina's wedding party in Ensenada. So let me summarize:

The bus ride was uneventful until we got close to Tecate, when the front left wheel began wobbling badly. To offset this the driver pulled over sharply in the other direction and hit a boulder with his front right which blew out the tire and bent the axle as well. Fortunately he had slowed down for a school crossing so no one was hurt, but the bus was seriously disabled. A gang of *campesinos* joined the passengers in ramming a telephone pole under the bus and trying to lever it back into an upright position. This didn't work. The driver, who had gone to a telephone, reported back that a new bus was leaving Tijuana as soon as lunch-break was over and it would be along in *un ratito* to pick us up; but, as the passengers were all Mexicans, they had heard this sort of thing too many times before, so most of us took our luggage and walked into Tecate each to fend for himself.

In Tecate I met a man who offered to take me across the U.S. border hidden in a truckload of adobe bricks for $300, and when I told him I was going in the opposite direction, with true Mexican flexibility he proposed taking me by the back road to Ensenada for only US $10 if I would drive most of the way as he had been on an all-night *fiesta* and didn't trust his reflexes on the mountain curves. I took him up on it and two hours later arrived in Ensenada. By rights he should have paid *me*, as he slept all the way and I did all the work, but I was so happy to be back in Mexico that I couldn't possibly quarrel over his little scam.

I took a taxi to the address Mamá had given me. It was at the end of a long dirt road that wound up into the hills back of the town. "It's up there somewhere," the cabbie said, dropping me a hundred meters short of my goal—he didn't care to risk his taxi on the final grade. So, with tennis racquets and bags, I walked to the top. The house was perched on a ledge with a view of *la ensenada* in both directions. It was very grand, or would be if it was ever finished. For now, the ground floor was built, and above it steel reinforcing rods pointed into the sky giving a suggestion of all the magnificence yet to come. The front of the house had a Grecian colonnade and a frieze in plaster of open eyes and pyramids, symbols of the Freemason order of which my brother-in-law-to-be was a fervent member. The yard was littered with debris, concrete blocks, form lumber and gravel, and in the driveway there was a dirty GMC flatbed, rolls of wire, a cement mixer and two upended wheelbarrows. It was quite a mess.

Marcantonio himself was sitting on the porch with a *ballena* of beer. He was unshaven, slightly tipsy and a lot flabbier than I remembered him. He didn't look much like the multi-billionaire (in pesos) young businessman I had met with Chele in Mexico City. Nor was my greeting exactly what I had expected.

"What are *you* doing here, little brother?" he asked. He didn't offer to shake my hand.

"I've come all the way across North America for the *fiesta*," I said proudly.

"*Jesumaria*! What *fiesta*?"

"For the wedding. For the *fiesta* of the wedding."

His face, none too amiable to start with, grew even cloudier. He jumped to his feet and yelled, "Fermin! Isidro! Come out here, you sons of bitches!"

His brothers instantly appeared in the front door. Fermin was very fat and Isidro had a black beard—I knew from my sister that he did pastel portraits for tourists on the Avenida Lopez Mateos. They glared at me without any sign of hospitality.

"Isidro! Fermin! You are my witnesses," Marcantonio

said with passion. "This son of a squid has come here to insult me."

I said hotly that I had done nothing of the sort, and that I was in Ensenada to represent the family at his wedding. To which I added that he was drunk and perhaps I should come back when he sobered up.

"Drunk?" he roared. "Of course I am drunk! Before God I ask if ever a man had more right to be drunk? Fermin! Isidro! You are my witnesses. Do I have the right—no, the *duty*—to be drunk? Shouldn't I be a hundred times drunk? Shouldn't I fill the bay out there with tequila and swallow it in one gulp? Tell the truth! Testify, you sons of bitches, testify!"

His brothers nodded their agreement.

"He wants to know where his whore of a sister is. As if he didn't know! As if he hadn't—" But he never finished that sentence because I struck him in the face and knocked him backward off the porch into a pile of planks. In a rage I leapt after him and began punching and kicking him.

"Help! Help!" Marcantonio screamed. "He's trying to kill me! Don Belisario sent him here to kill me!" (*Don Belisario* is my father on important occasions.)

But the brothers didn't stir. Either they thought Marcantonio deserved what he got or they just in general enjoyed a fight, I don't know which. Meanwhile, a number of startled women and children ran out to watch.

Marcantonio was really no match for me in my fury. He is bigger than I am but fat and out of shape. So the instant he could get free of my fists he ran around the cement mixer, grabbed a heavy shovel and charged at me swinging it around his head.

"I'll kill the son of a squid," he roared.

But his brothers thought matters had gone far enough.

"No, you won't," said the black-bearded one and stuck out one foot, causing Marcantonio to trip and fall flat on his face. Then he jumped on his back and twisted his arm in a hammer-lock.

At the same instant the fat brother fell on me—quite literally *fell*—knocking the wind out of me. He then sat on me, all 150 kilos of him.

The children began laughing, and pretty soon the triumphant peace-makers joined in.

When I heard that laughter all the rage and anger drained out of me.

"No more fighting?" the fat brother asked.

I grunted my assent.

"Then I'll let you up." He got off me and offered a hand to help me to my feet, a hand which I refused.

But Brother Isidro still kept his hammerlock on Marcantonio. He pulled him to a sitting posture and we could all hear his sobbing; it silenced everyone.

"I built this house for her," Marcantonio said through his tears. "It was for her . . . a present for her."

"Love is a terrible master," Isidro said softly. "Look. He's weeping. Go inside, children, this doesn't concern you."

Reluctantly, the children left the scene while Isidro explained to me that my sister Chele had announced two weeks ago that the wedding was off and that she was taking a job in Sinaloa. "She's working for a travel agency in Los Mochis," Fermin added. "Taking tourists to look at the Tarahumaro Indians. What could be more foolish?"

"Let me go," Marcantonio sobbed.

"He has been like this for two weeks," the artist brother said. "We moved in here because we were afraid to leave him alone."

"Yes," said Marcantonio grimly, "they thought I would kill myself. And I would have, too, if I weren't such a contemptible coward."

"Shut up!" Fermin said, "before you make me puke."

"Let me go! You're breaking my arm." His brother somewhat tentatively loosened his grip and Marcantonio staggered to his feet and confronted me.

"Did Don Belisario send you?"

"I haven't seen my father in two years," I said.

"Then you didn't know?"

"How could I? I've been playing tennis matches in the United States. I haven't heard from anyone since the beginning of summer."

Dramatically, Marcantonio struck himself on the forehead. "Fool! Idiot!" he shouted. "You've done it again! You drove her away with your stupid jealousy, and now you strike her innocent little brother. Marcantonio Rodriguez, you are a pig—no, worse than that, a *mono*, an ape!"

"Shut your bawling," Fermin yelled. "You make me sick!"

But Marcantonio ignored him and turned his tear-stained face to me. "Forgive me, little brother," he pleaded. "I love her more than anything else in the world—that's why I unjustly insulted you. My heart is broken, don't you see? I am *loco*—I don't know what I'm doing. Say you forgive me—out of pity for a miserable *loco* if for nothing else."

"Go on, say you forgive him," Isidro said. "It will let him sleep. And us, too."

"I'm sick of his wailing," Fermin added. "Forgive him before I puke all over him."

So I said I forgave Marcantonio.

"Thank you, little brother, thank you!" he cried and tried to seize my hand which I managed to keep out of his reach.

"Let's go into the house now," Fermin suggested. "The women are cooking a goat—we'll have some *birría*. I can smell it from here."

"And I'll play my guitar," Isidro said. "Perhaps some *flamenco?*"

"No," I said. "I forgive him because of his grief. But I cannot enter his house after what he has said about my sister and my father."

"Forget it," said the fat brother. "That's all water under the bridge."

"No," said the bearded brother. "I understand Agosto's feelings. I would act the same myself. The honor of his family is at stake. But you must drink with us before you go. *Our* honor requires it."

"All right," I said, brushing the cement dust from my new jacket. "One drink." I did not dare tell them how much I disliked tequila—under the circumstances it might have started a new round of insults.

"To the revolution," Isidro said, tipping the bottle.

"And the counter-revolution," said his brother in turn.

"To friendship," I proposed.

Marcantonio drank and said nothing.

The scorching sun beat down on us all, poor fools, as we stood on that scarred and disfigured hill overlooking the azure blue of the Pacific, the *peaceful* sea, as Nuñez de Balboa had called it, and passed the tequila bottle from hand to hand and swore like good Mexicans to let the past die in the past and rejoice in the living present. I felt at peace as I had not for many long months. Honor had been satisfied, I had acted the man, and, best of all, I had crossed the border and found my true home again.

What Happened Afterward

Six months have passed. I am back in Montevideo, playing tennis every morning with Uncle Pablo Uriarte, my coach and my father's old friend from Spain. He says my game has gone downhill. "Too much Yankee pussy," is his explanation. He has me running to the right on every one of his shots so that I will have to return everything backhand. It takes more strength to take hard-hit ground strokes on the backhand and he thinks this stratagem will build me up. My game obviously needs improving; in my absence I have slid right off the computer and am no longer ranked. Uncle Pablo plans to remedy that by entering me in a number of regional South American tournaments. I do as he tells me. After all, he knows what he is talking about; I am not so sure any more that I do.

Last week I got a letter from Taos, New Mexico. It was from Phyllis Holiwell. She wanted to thank me for my sympathy and support during her "time of crisis." She was opening a new sculpture show in Minneapolis the following month and then planned to fly to Venice for something she called the "Biennale"; whether it was a party or an exhibition I couldn't make out. At the end of her letter she asked me to put on Albert's weaving, read the letter again and "concentrate on your inmost thoughts." "Wherever I am at that moment," she concluded, "I know there will be a *frisson*. Do this for me, Agosto, I need the spiritual impulse which only you and Albert can provide." I hadn't worn Albert's *sarape* at all in Montevideo—if people here see you in one they think you an American hippie—but I did as Phyllis asked and felt an unmistakable mystic presence. It was weak at first, but the mandala still gave off vibrations—the old magic was not utterly dead.

I have an apartment here in a modern high-rise on the Avenida Veinte-y-Cinco de Agosto. It is small and on the *1er piso* over a surfer's shop, but it has all the conveniences, the address is semi-fashionable, and, best of all, I have it virtually rent free. How this came about is worth recounting.

I had been back in Uruguay a couple of weeks when I decided to call on Mr. Petronelli of the Banco Agripecuario, who, as you will remember, was a fellow board director of mine. I had some business cards printed up with my name and, very simply, in one corner, the firm name of Llanas Llenas, S.A. I called at bank headquarters and had my card sent in. It was truly amazing with what celerity Mr. Petronelli had me ushered in. He gave me a cordial *abrazo* and began *tu*-ing me from the moment I introduced myself. After a couple of phone calls a meeting was set up for the next day at the very exclusive Montevideo Jockey Club.

Here I was introduced to a Mr. Fagundes, the Secretary of Llanas Llenas, S.A., and a Colonel Silva who, I was told, was the personal representative of the political leader I have called Mr. Z—. The gentlemen took brandies, while I had a Perrier and lime juice. Col. Silva was particularly impressive; he had silver white hair and moustaches although otherwise quite trim and youthful and was in the full dress uniform of the National Guard.

All three gentlemen asked me searching if friendly questions. Naturally, they were curious as to how I—a financial novice—had come to be a board member of two international corporations. I explained that I had been an innocent *prestanombre* and they seemed to believe me. Col. Silva asked about Mr. Wetherall, with whom he had had earlier dealings in Buenos Aires. Were he and his accountant really such big crooks as the U.S. police now maintained? Who had shot Mr. Wetherall and why? Were criminal indictments likely? If so, who would be involved, now that the two principals were dead? I answered that Messrs. Wetherall and Holiwell had always been honest and forthright in their dealings with me. I gave them what details I could of Mr. Wetherall's death and my own theory that rival shrimp dealers may have been behind it. I then told them about Mr. Phil Fogarty and his proposed law suits and described the proposals he had made me and how I had resisted them. Throughout all this I tried to be as candid as I possibly could. I was on thin ice, I knew—the slightest hint of a threat to men as powerful and sophisticated as these would be absolutely fatal. I could disappear without a trace. Or, like a number of other imprudent persons I had heard of, my body, neatly wrapped in sacking, could be dredged up in some purseseiner's net in the Rio de la Plata.

However, the financiers at the Jockey Club continued smiling and affable; they seemed no end pleased with my conduct.

"Young man," the Colonel said benignly, "you have acted like a good Uruguayan in refusing to become involved in any such litigation as these Yankee lawyers suggest."

I said that my first thought when confronted by Mr. Fogarty's demands had been for our national honor.

At this Mr. Fagundes, a sharp-eyed little man who wore the rosette of the Legion of Honor, gave me a dubious glance, but Col. Silva's approval was immediate and over-riding.

"Of course, of course! In the face of such insulting

proposals you took absolutely the correct line of action. Immediate and unconditional departure. That was the only way open to you to answer a slur on the national honor."

Mr. Petronelli agreed. He also pointed out that I had been a member of the Uruguayan Davis Cup squad. "I am sure," he said, "that Mr. Villaseñor well knows how to represent the Uruguayan flag when abroad."

I too agreed and thanked them for their confidence in me. I then announced that, with my mission concluded, I thought it best to submit my resignation from Llanas Llenas, S.A., effective at once.

They all agreed on the wisdom and generosity of this offer and with that our meeting broke up, though not without many more *abrazos* and friendly wishes.

However, when I went into Mr. Fagundes's office the next morning to sign the resignation papers I was informed of a change of plans.

"Sign the documents, please," Mr. Fagundes instructed me, "but don't fill in the date. The board has decided that, as a representative of the new generation of Uruguayans, you should remain a member—for the time being. Your insights will no doubt be of great value."

I saw at once that he didn't believe this last at all and that I owed my continuing career in finance to Col. Silva and Mr. Petronelli, but naturally I didn't let him know it.

"I hope I shall be worthy of the honor," I said, choking up a little. Mr. Fagundes nodded briefly and did not offer the customary congratulatory *abrazo*. For which I was grateful—his breath was heavy with garlic.

The very next day the apartment became available; Mr. Petronelli owned the building and would be glad to let me have it if once every week or so I would go over the concierge's accounts and keep an eye on his expenditures which had lately shown signs of extravagance. And the following week I got a job of sorts. It didn't pay a lot but then the duties—inspecting incoming Black Angus cattle for the agriculture department—didn't amount to much either. On average, there were only three incoming cattle-boats a month and it was understood that if I should be on tour I could hire a clerk to check the invoices.

So, as you can see, I am still essentially only a *prestanombre*, although I have shifted sides and now stand for the national honor against foreign interference. There are perks, too—Col. Silva is proposing me for membership in the Jockey Club and I have just received two tickets for the presidential inaugural ball. Of course, there are times when I feel as if I were selling myself, but then it seems unlikely that I will ever make much of a living playing tennis and I will have to sell my time and talents in one direction or another, so why not here? And when I meditate—usually with Albert's *sarape* over my shoulders—it often comes to me that this is my guru's true gift to me, this the real reward of my arduous travels through America.

Tomorrow I have to be at the airport to pick up a visitor—Miss Victoria-Evangeline Moore. Yes, Vicki is coming to Montevideo for a visit. Her letter didn't say for how long but I hope at least for a few weeks. She doesn't have to be back right away as she is no longer working for Sunset Estates. It seems Mr. Wilder Fawcett is under indictment on suspicion of smuggling cocaine and the Chinese partners have taken over complete control of his various projects. Vicki reports that Mr. Fawcett is free on bail and "a lot less hyper," whatever that means.

The great thing about Victoria is that she's always there making a real effort to be helpful when you need her. Friendship to her means *giving*. I like that. Perhaps it's because she has already done her growing up and now, at thirty, she knows what she wants and can concentrate on getting it.

And Sabrina? I knew you would ask that. At last report Sabrina was in Madagascar working at saving the rain forests. Next year she wants to meet me in Manaos on the Amazon. *Quién sabe?* All that is in the future.

Just as I was about to finish this the *cartero* blew his familiar little whistle and there, under the door, was a letter from Mamá. I had clipped the Inaugural Ball guest list out of the paper and sent it to her to show that, contrary to all her predictions, I was coming up in the world. To which she responded that under no circumstances was I to attend, as the rental of a dress suit would surely cost me a month's salary. Her other reports were equally gloomy. Papá was still number one on the list to be promoted wine steward at Mr. Hyatt's, but now he was getting arthritis in his left wrist and the pain was so bad that he had to carry his tray with the wrong hand which had led to some awkward accidents and she didn't know how much longer the poor man could continue. Sergio had just been confirmed and his brother was in trouble for stealing consecrated wafers from the church. As for sister Celestina, Mamá had heard from her but almost wished she hadn't. The idiotic girl had thrown up her good job in Los Mochis and gone back to Marcantonio. Now she wrote that they were finishing their house in Ensenada and everything between them was fine as long as they kept off the subject of weddings. Chele swore that she would never, *never* get married and Mamá said that was just as well because nobody in our family would come to the wedding.

I certainly know I wouldn't.